Jake Harwood

Harvey Mendez

Mendez, Harvey
ISBN: 9798645762407
Jake Harwood / Harvey Mendez – 1st ed.

Cover art by Mark Patterson
Edited by Pat Oplinger

Printed in the USA

Jake Harwood

Dedication:

Thanks to Ann, my wife, and to Pat Oplinger,
my editor, for all their help.
Also, thanks to The Cherokee Village Writers Group
and to The Lagunita Writers Group.

CHAPTER ONE

Jake Harwood eased his large buckskin over the last ridge before the wide expanse of the New Mexico backcountry began. He had been on the trail out of Santa Fe for five weeks and was dusty and tired. The Rio Grande, with its cool and soothing water, was some distance behind and Sam, his horse, needed water. He started downhill as the sky turned copper, but reined to a quick halt. A cloud of dust, vanishing in the southwest, caught his eye. Reaching into his left saddlebag, he pulled out a small field glass and peered through the lens. A band of Apache braves raced their ponies into the afternoon sun. Jake scanned the area next to the trail that parted the plains. An overturned stagecoach lay half-buried in the sand.

Urging his horse forward past clumps of brush and cactus, Jake drew his gun and cautiously trotted toward the stage. The bright sun and a slight breeze brushed his face. He adjusted his hat. Nothing moved as he drew closer. The coach was tipped on its side and the driver lay slumped over a wheel. A dead guard lay face up in front of the stage with an arrow protruding from his chest. All six horses had been cut loose. Three passengers, with arrows in their backs, lay spread-eagled, face down, in the soft sand next to the coach's door. Their bloody scalps attracted hungry ants. Trunks and baggage, busted open, lay scattered around and the strong box was smashed and empty.

Jake shifted his blue eyes from the bodies and dismounted from his horse. He flinched when he heard a scraping sound.

"Here . . . Help! Please . . . Help!" A choked cry belched from underneath the dug-in coach.

"Hold on." Jake ran to the other side of the stage.

The sand shifted by the half-buried door. He dug with his large hands. The back of a woman's head popped up first, then her hands and arms fought for freedom. She winced, shook her long, brown hair, and gasped for breath.

"Thank heaven!" She spit out sand and dirt clogged in her throat.

"You all right?" Jake stared at the encased young woman.

"I—I think so . . . ooowww!" She tried to wiggle out of her tomb, but the sharp pain in her left shoulder kept her captive.

"Let me help you. Just sit still a minute." Jake bent down, scooped out more sand from around her lower body. "There— that should do it, but don't move yet." He wrapped his arms under her breasts and slowly tugged her out of the hole.

"Who—who are you?" She rested against his chest.

"Jake—Jake Harwood."

"My arm hurts." She tried to move it.

"Take it easy." He released her. "I'll get water."

She sagged against the stagecoach. After a few swallows of water, the dazed woman looked over the carnage. "Horrible! Are they all dead?" She gingerly brushed dirt and sand off her dress with her good hand.

"Yeah, they're dead." Jake poured a little water from his canteen onto his weathered bandanna and handed it to her.

She squeezed the cloth, wiped it across her forehead, around her eyes, and down her cheeks. After patting her lips and neck with the scarf, she bent her head and shook the grit from her hair. Wincing, she grabbed her shoulder. "I must have bruised this more than I thought."

"Might be broken. Let me see." Jake gently felt her shoulder, then folded his bandanna into a sling and fitted her arm into it.

The woman stood slowly. "That feels better." They faced each other for a moment without speaking.

He saw her beauty through all the dirt and anguish, but just stood and stared.

She gazed at his handsome ruggedness. "I guess I should introduce myself, and thank you properly. I'm Jessica. Jessica Raymond."

"Glad to meet you, ma'am."

"It's Miss . . ."

"What are you doing in Indian Territory?"

2

"I'm from New Orleans. I was on my way to California when . . ." She snapped back to what had just happened. Moving away from Jake, she surveyed the bodies strewn about the stagecoach. "I didn't realize Indians were this brutal." She covered her eyes.

"Apaches are raiders." Jake checked the victims again. "You are fortunate. They usually scalp and dismember the bodies." He scanned the scene. "Nothing we can do for these poor souls."

Jessica shuddered, put a hand to her mouth. "Shouldn't we bury them?"

"Got to tell the sheriff first."

"Why did they attack us?" She looked away from the bloody site.

"Probably for the horses . . . and gold. The cash box was empty."

"How would they know there was gold?" She still cringed at what had happened.

Jake looked closely at her. "I don't know, but we'd better get into town. Adobe Crossing isn't far."

"What about my things?" Jessica turned now, scanned the scattered luggage. Her fashionable trunk was still intact. "There." She pointed.

"Your trunk will have to wait. It'll be dark soon." He helped her up on his horse.

The afternoon sun lowered on the horizon and the desert's eerie shadows danced around them. The buckskin handled his double load easily over the grooved, worn trail toward the small town. Neither person spoke much, but Jake's curiosity peaked about the pretty lady from New Orleans pressing against him in the saddle.

CHAPTER TWO

Soon after dark, Jake and Jessica entered Adobe Crossing, a sleepy little Mexican village before Americans took over the town after the Mexican War. Main Street housed a block-long merchant district plus the sheriff's office. A livery stable stood at the town's entrance and a gambling hall at the western end of the street.

They rode past the stores and reined up in front of the jail. Jessica dismounted first and headed for the door. Jake tied Sam to the post out front.

Jessica burst into the jail. "Sheriff! . . . we need your help! My stagecoach was attacked by Apaches!"

Sheriff John Ramos, in his forties, medium height, with a full head of graying hair, looked up from his desk. "Apaches? How do you know they were Apaches?"

"Because I told her." Jake entered, closed the door behind him.

"And who are you?" The lawman rose from his chair.

"Jake Harwood. And this is Jessica Raymond. They took horses and gold. Left several dead bodies and an overturned stage. Miss Raymond was the only survivor. I just happened along."

The sheriff turned to Jessica. "Sorry you had to witness such horror, Miss."

"Thank you." Her face looked pained, like she would faint. "It was terrible."

"It's too dark to go out there now, but my men and I will bring in the bodies at first light." The sheriff sat down.

"Thanks, Sheriff." Jake observed Jessica. "I better get you to the hotel."

Jessica turned. "Yes, I'm done in."

Jake untied Sam and led him across the street to the hotel. He checked them in at the desk and the clerk gave them separate keys.

"You go on up to your room," Jake said. "I'll meet you at the dining room after I bed Sam down for the night at the livery stable."

"All right." Jessica started for the stairs. "I'm famished. Haven't eaten much."

"Yeah, me too. A big steak will set just right." He tipped his hat and headed out the door.

Jake came back to the hotel a short time later. Jessica was seated at a table in the dining room. He beat the dust off his hat and shirt and joined her.

She looked up. "Hello. Is your horse all settled?"

"Yeah. He was hungry too."

The saloonkeeper's helper took their order and they sat back and relaxed a bit.

"Quite a day," he said.

"Yes. Don't want any more like this. Still see the brutality."

Their food came and they ate without much more conversation. When finished, they walked up the stairs to their rooms.

"See you in the morning." Jake stopped at his door.

"Good night, Jake. And thank you for saving me."

Jake slowly opened his eyes and squinted in the early morning sunlight that streaked through the porous shade covering the window. He looked around the modest room with its pale-green walls that needed patching. Rising, he splashed water from a basin into his sleepy eyes and on his face. Freshened, he dried with a towel from a nearby hook. After he finished dressing and strapped on his gunbelt, he pulled the Colt .44 and checked the chamber.

Jessica awoke from her restless sleep to the sounds of horses and wagons clattering down the street. She slipped from her bed and peered out the window. The sheriff and his men unloaded baggage and bodies from the stagecoach massacre. She stared down for a moment, then sat back on the bed and put her face in her hands. The last four weeks flashed through her mind. *Her father's death . . . Blackie Le Font . . . the Apaches' butchery . . . and now—the tall Jake Harwood. She had wanted to get as far west as possible, maybe California. She'd have to find a way.*

Jake stood by his door. *He'd better see if Jessica was up. He needed to load supplies and get going today. He still felt her soft warmth on his back. The thought of leaving her shook him.* He opened the door and walked down the hall.

Jessica opened her door after the second knock.

"Morning." He pulled his arm back. "How did you sleep?"

She looked away. "Not very well. I kept waking, hearing all the screams and seeing the carnage from yesterday."

"I'm sure it was quite a shock, but that's the way it is in the west sometimes."

"Don't think I'll ever get over it. Had never seen so much blood."

"I hope you do." He motioned. "Would you like some breakfast now?"

"Yes, I'll be ready in a minute."

Jake leaned against the door jam. "I think I'll head out on the trail today."

Jessica raised her head. "I'd like to talk to you about that."

"Fine—at the breakfast table."

"All right." She squeezed past him.

They walked down the stairs, smelled coffee and flapjacks from the dining room, and ordered breakfast. Jake ate a much heartier meal than Jessica. She finished first and watched him while having more coffee.

"My," she said, "you seem to have a healthy appetite."

"Yes, I do this morning. I'd been on the trail for some time on my way to California before I came across you and the stage."

"Where did you come from?"

"Wichita—Dodge City, where I hooked up with the Santa Fe Trail. Dodge is a booming town, but I only stayed long enough to pick up supplies. After the Pecos River, I went on to

Santa Fe and rested a few days before heading into Indian Territory."

"Well, I'm glad you found me when you did." She sipped her coffee. "I was on my way west, too. I just didn't know how far I'd get."

"California's about as far west as you can go."

"I know." She looked him straight in the eye. "Would you consider taking me with you?"

Jake pulled back. "I don't know . . . hadn't planned on any company."

"I wouldn't be any trouble." Her voice was soft and confident. "I can ride and take care of myself." Then she looked away. "Blackie found that out . . ."

"Who's Blackie?"

"No one important, any more. Maybe I'll explain it to you on the trail."

He stopped eating. "Wait a minute, I didn't say you could come."

"Oh, please, Jake. It's a long way to California. Two people can survive better than one."

"I don't know. We just met. Lots of things could happen."

"Lots of things have already happened." She stared into his eyes again. "I may have killed someone."

Jake pushed back from the table. "Oh—let me guess— Blackie."

"Yes—but I had to."

"I see. Is the law after you?"

"I don't know. Please take me with you."

"Maybe, but you won't be able to take that trunk of yours."

"That's all right. That part of my life is over anyway."

"Okay, we'll try it."

"Oh, thank you. You won't regret it, Jake. I promise."

"I hope not." He moved back to the table and took a last gulp of coffee. "Best we get over to the sheriff's office and see if they brought in your trunk. I'm sure you'll need a few things out of it."

The sheriff told them the victims' bodies were at the funeral parlor next to the jailhouse. Jessica went through her trunk for underclothes and blouses then offered her fine dresses and other valuables to the town's needy. The sheriff thanked her.

Jake checked them out of the hotel and ordered flour, sugar, coffee, and other supplies at the general store. They went to the livery stable where Jake found a sturdy brown and white pinto mustang for Jessica. He outfitted the horse with a bedroll behind her saddle and stuffed a carbine in a sheath on the right side of the saddle.

His horse, Sam, was fed, watered, saddled, and ready to go.

Jessica went to the general store, bought riding britches, boots, and a trail hat.

"Looks like we're ready to go." Jake met her outside the store.

They mounted their horses and set out west from Adobe Crossing.

The first night out, the two riders camped beside a small stream sheltered on the east side by a single hill with plenty of grass. Jessica cooked beans and roasted a small quail, Jake had shot, on the campfire. Hungry, they ate without much conversation, but each watched the other.

Jake finished first and cleaned his plate in the stream. *He was still wary about bringing Jessica along, but she seemed to hold up okay the first day. She carried herself with an air of confidence and this fairly tall woman with dark brown hair that flowed beneath her hat stirred his emotions. She was pretty with soft brown eyes and medium sized breasts. He hadn't thought about another woman since his wife, Ella, left him.*

Jessica looked up when she heard Jake walking back to camp. *Here she was with this handsome, tall, raw-boned man on the trail to California. He wasn't a bit like Blackie and didn't say too much, but she was thankful he had saved her from the Apaches. Maybe, little by little, they'd get to know one another.* She cleaned her utensils and came back to open bedrolls placed between their saddles and the hearty fire.

"That'll keep the coyotes away." Jake pointed to the flames.

"Good. Thank you. I think we should get some sleep."

"Yes." He loosened his gunbelt, but kept it close to his head when he lay down.

"Good night, Jake," Jessica said.

"Good night."

The next morning, Jake woke first and made coffee before he awakened Jessica. After breakfast of biscuits and gravy, they continued on their way.

"Well, this is our second day," Jake said, "do you want to tell me about this Blackie you said you might've killed?"

Jessica tugged her reins, looked a little surprised at his abruptness. "It's a rather long story—starts with my father, Arthur Raymond. You sure you want to hear it?"

Jake slowed his horse also. "Yes, I'm very interested."

She felt heat on her cheeks, but not from the sun. "Father sailed to New Orleans from England. He was a merchant, but sought a new land and a new start in life. He wasn't very successful in England. Mother died when I was eight years old and that also triggered his decision to come to America. He started a haberdashery and was a good father for a few years, but when the business didn't prosper enough he left me on my own more and more. He never told me where he went, but I followed him once and found out he was gambling. He hoped it would bring him an easy fortune."

"And you were only about nine years old?" Jake asked. "I imagine that was quite a shock."

"It was. I didn't know what to do. That's when he met Blackie Le Font, who owned Blackie's Saloon and Gambling Hall. Father was an impeccable dresser and Blackie gave him substantial credit and encouraged him to gamble. We lived in the best hotels, but New Orleans society shunned Father because he wasn't respectable in their eyes. At first he started winning big at the tables, but the more he won the more he drank and soon he began losing large sums of money."

"Did he ever suspect Blackie might have rigged the whole thing?"

"I don't know. Father gambled so much he didn't know what he was doing."

"How old were you then?"

"I had just turned eighteen when the debts piled up so high Father only had the shop left. Blackie kept extending him credit, but forced him to sign over the shop. I saw less and less of Father. One night, he became so desperate he cheated in a poker game. Blackie caught him and shot him. I buried him in the public cemetery."

Jake looked at Jessica as she wiped the tears from her eyes. "I guess you had it pretty rough. Did they put Blackie away?"

"No. He claimed self-defense. All the witnesses said Father drew his Derringer first. Blackie was a powerful man."

"Was? Do you really think you killed him?"

"I'd better finish the story. Ever since I turned about fourteen, Blackie's been after me. He even brought flowers to the funeral, asked me out to dinner, said I could work for him—invented ways to see me."

Jake scratched his forehead. "I can understand his interest."

Jessica blushed. "Maybe, but I couldn't do it. I despised him so. He wanted me to move in to his hotel and work off Father's debts. He used all his charms to persuade me to marry him. Then I thought up a plan to repay him for what he'd done to my father. Despite all his weaknesses, I loved Father deeply."

"So, did you marry Blackie?"

Jessica raised her eyebrows. "No, I told him I'd come up to his suite one night and talk about an arrangement. I put on a very seductive dress and met him. He was quite cordial and after a couple of drinks, I offered myself to him in exchange for all my father's markers. While eyeing my low-cut gown, he thought it over a few minutes and then agreed to the conditions. When he turned to open the safe and remove the papers, I pulled out a pistol from my handbag and clubbed him over the head. He dropped to the floor and didn't move. I thought I'd killed him. I grabbed the markers, lit a match to them, and set the whole place on fire. The flames spread so quickly I ran down the back stairs—didn't look back. Early the next morning, I packed my trunk and boarded the westbound stage."

Jake reined Sam to a halt. "That's some story."

"And then you found me." She sighed and pushed back her hat.

At noon, they rested by a group of rocks in a narrow gully and fed their horses on bush grass growing nearby.

Jake leaned against a rock and watched Jessica. *She could withstand their journey now. She was solid stock, a whole woman he's never known. Bold, not afraid, yet not overbearing like some of the stuffy females he'd seen in Wichita. The kind who wanted the town safe, but shuddered each time he strapped on his gun.*

They started out again and Jessica opened up again. "You know, I feel I should own a hotel, after all the years I lived in one. Takes a lot of hard work and money to start. Don't know about gambling—Father's experiences are hard to forget."

"Well, maybe we'll get lucky in the gold fields." Jake urged Sam to a trot. "I'd like to cover some ground before dark today."

CHAPTER THREE

Blackie Le Font smelled the smoke first, then heard the flames crackling. He stirred, opened his dark eyes to blurriness, and attempted to lift his throbbing head. Pain shot through him like hailstones pelting the ground. Still not certain what happened, he touched his thick black hair and felt the large lump protruding from his scalp. "Owww." He slipped back into the grogginess and lay spread out on the rug in front of his empty safe.

A short time later, Blackie stirred; his senses returned. He shook his head, raised on his elbows, and gazed at the safe. "That tramp—she cleaned me out."

Heavy black smoke rapidly filled his plush parlor. The far side of the room was ablaze and he tasted the intense heat scorching his face. Screams echoed from the gambling hall below. He pulled himself up on the desk's corner, but choked on the smoke. Dropping to his knees, he crawled to the window overlooking the back alley. Then he braced against the blue velvet couch, kicked, shattered the window, and tumbled through the opening onto the balcony.

Once outside, Blackie saw the fire had engulfed the entire upstairs of the hotel. Flames shot upward, climbing the roof like a ladder. "That bitch!" He slid down a support post. "She won't get away with this."

He staggered to the front of the saloon just as the horses and fire brigade came to a noisy halt. Too late. The elegant structure could not be saved. Blackie stood wide-eyed and enraged by the destruction. "I'll kill her."

The next day, Blackie stared at the smoldering ruins. *He'd find her if it took forever.*

He called in his outstanding markers after he found out Jessica had taken the stage to Santa Fe. With his horse, Ace, he boarded a northbound riverboat and proceeded west along the Red River.

After supper, their fourth day out, Jake and Jessica sat beside the fire drinking coffee. *He marveled at the young, New Orleans beauty who shunned her elegant dresses that filled her trunk and donned the practical britches that graced her slim body. She seemed so completely opposite of Ella. He definitely was attracted to her.*

Jessica interrupted his thoughts. "Do you want to hear more of my story?"

Jake stirred. "Yeah, go on."

"Well, I never had much schooling as a kid. Father was always in such bad condition I couldn't attend classes much. And I didn't have the fine clothes required by the New Orleans elite. Picked up most of my education at hotels, watching and learning, from refusing men who made advances, to running the place. That's why I said I should own a hotel. Knew one man when I was older—a sea captain from France. My first love, but he was killed off the coast of Africa. Haven't met another like him."

Jake held up his right hand. "You amaze me. You're not the dainty woman I expected when I dug you out from beneath that stagecoach."

"Don't know what you thought, but I do know I can keep up with you on this trip. Unless the Apaches change our plans."

"That may be our biggest problem. They don't like us here."

"Why do they hate us so?"

"Once this was all Apache land. First, the Spanish, then the Mexicans, then the Americans violated these deserts and mountains. The Apaches are great warriors. I heard their leader, Cochise, a Chiricahua Apache, welcomed the Americans when the first settlers arrived. That paved the way for the Butterfield Overland Mail to set up a stage station in Apache Pass. But it all changed when a Lieutenant George Bascom of the Seventh Infantry hanged Cochise's brother and two nephews at Apache Pass. Then the Apaches became guerrilla fighters. Cochise joined up with Mangas Colorado, a seventy-year-old Mimbreno Apache, who happened to be Cochise's wife's father. Together they drove the Americans from their homeland. Even the Mexican Government offered three hundred dollars for each Apache scalp."

Jessica's face livened with passion. "I don't blame them. I would fight, too."

"Well, let's hope we don't have to."

The campfire burned low now. Jake gathered more wood and sat next to Jessica as the flames rose again.

Jessica felt the warmth and moved closer to Jake. "Why did you decide to come west and seek gold?"

"I'm not quite sure. I was a lawman once. Maybe the townspeople had a lot to do with it." *He didn't know if he should tell her about the men he'd killed to stay alive or about Ella. He tried to blank out the morning Ella told him she was leaving.* "I grew up in Missouri. My dad taught me how to shoot before I was ten. Then he died when I was eighteen. I left home and worked my way to Wichita using my gun."

"Is that why you don't talk much about it now?"

"That's right, but you're easy to talk to."

"Thank you."

"Wichita was still wide open when I arrived. Many marshals had come and gone before me. Got into a gunfight with a young drunk. Tried to talk him out of it, but I had to kill him. Witnesses told the acting marshal what happened and he offered me a job. I was a deputy for four years before I became the U. S. Marshal. The next year, I met Ella Wells."

"Was she your wife?" Jessica shifted her eyes from the fire to Jake's face.

Jake stared into the darkness. "Yes. I still remember the day she left . . ."

CHAPTER FOUR

Marshal Jake Harwood had just ridden down Wichita's main street and reined up in front of the General Store. He dismounted and walked up the steps. Ella Wells turned, stared at the handsome, six-foot-two-inch lawman. He stood in the doorway, his muscular frame adorned with a bandoleer, half full of cartridges and a Bowie knife attached to the left side of his gunbelt opposite the Colt .44 worn high on his waist.

Ella, twenty-four years old, had come west from New England because she did not want to marry the man her parents picked out for her. Her minister father reluctantly let her go to the frontier. Her mother was silent.

Jake returned her stare. She had a soft, pretty face with light brown eyes, a slender figure, long sandy hair, and an infectious smile. Ella realized she was smiling and turned away. She felt the heat within and picked up a fan.

Jake watched her fan herself; a slight grin creased his lips. *Now there's a woman.*

Ella sneaked a peek at him. *He was watching her. She had not known any man physically, but the sensation she felt aroused her in a special way.*

The spark between them clicked and soon Ella, who lived in a small house her dead brother owned at the edge of town, invited Jake for a visit. They courted for a couple of months before Jake asked her to marry him. After the wedding, Jake moved into her house and they settled down to married life. Every day, he practiced with his pistol in the backyard and became proficient with it and a Winchester rifle.

At first, Ella was happy and contented. Physically they enjoyed each other, but after the first year passed she worried more and more each time Jake went out the door to work. "You put in such long hours and somebody is always gunning for you."

"That's part of the job," Jake said. "You knew that when I met you."

Finally it happened. Three young gunmen called him out one day. He killed two of the men, but the other one shot Jake in the left arm. He whirled, shot the man in the chest.

One morning, Jake opened his eyes, looked around the bedroom, then nudged Ella. "Hey, wake up sleepyhead."

"Huh? Oh, good morning, darling."

The sun streamed into the room. Jake pulled Ella close and embraced her. She felt soft and warm. He tilted her head and kissed her tenderly. "I love you, Honey. Wish I didn't have to go in so early this morning."

"Me too. Stay with me."

"I'm sorry, but we've got a heavy load today. Sandy's bringing in the Parker Brothers for trial."

She sat up. "Jake, I must talk with you now."

"Can it wait until I get home?"

"No. I can't take it any longer. I'm afraid for you. Your gun-fighting reputation has grown too much. Some day you won't be lucky enough. Somebody will kill you."

"Ella, it's my job. I'm good at it. I love it."

She took a deep breath. "I know you do, but I'm frightened. Every time you leave the house it hurts, not knowing if you'll return."

Jake moved to the edge of the bed. "Three years from now we'll have enough money saved to buy a little ranch outside of town. I won't have to be a marshal."

"That won't change things. You're famous. We'll never have any real peace."

"I'm sorry, but I can't quit my job. When I first came here outlaws owned this town. My gun was the tamer."

She winced. "That's what I mean—your gun—I'm scared one day you won't come home. I want babies, a home, and a husband at my side every night. Maybe I should have stayed back east. My father might have been right."

Jake turned, put his hands on her shoulders. "How can you forget our good times? Especially the lovin'."

"I can't." Tears welled in her eyes. "I love you, Jake. When you touch me, kiss me, make love to me I'm completely yours, but I'm going to leave you. I have to."

Jake drew backward. "What? You're not serious?"

"I am serious. This last year—all the narrow escapes, the wounds, the silent anxiety I've gone through. The agony isn't worth it."

"I can't believe this. When you're in my arms everything is so natural. I never dreamed you felt like this."

"I do, though. I've made up my mind. I'm going back east."

"You're all that matters to me. I made this town safe for you, for our babies, and all the others. Stay, please stay. We'll talk later."

Ella folded her arms. "It's too late. I don't want this kind of life anymore. I need the kind of security your job will never provide."

Jake's face reddened slightly. He rose from the bed, buckled his gunbelt on his waist, and grabbed his low-brimmed hat. "So, that's it? That's final?"

"I'll be gone when you get back," Ella said.

Jake slammed the door. Ella sat in bed, stared at the emptiness, but could not hold back her tears . . . .

* * * *

Jake still stared into the darkness when Jessica stirred the campfire.

"So what happened after your wife left you?" she asked.

"Oh—sorry—guess I was off somewhere." He turned to her. "Killers came and went, but it wasn't the same without Ella. I went through the motions until I was confronted with a resolution from the townspeople. They wanted an end to the killing and gunplay. I told them they had a safe town, but they said gunmen would always seek me out. I thought maybe they were right. Ella was gone. I'd had enough fighting. Gold had been discovered in California. It was time to move on."

"Lucky for me you did." Jessica turned to him.

19

“Yeah, lucky.”

CHAPTER FIVE

Blackie Le Font walked his black stallion, Ace, down Adobe Crossing's main street. He was tired and wiped brown sweat off his brow. His black hat and suit were covered with dust and dirt from two weeks of hard riding on the trail. He took a chance that Jessica would take the southbound stagecoach from Santa Fe. His usually shiny black boots showed the scars of the desert as he dismounted in front of the sheriff's office. It was almost dark; the lantern on the lawman's desk flickered when he opened the door.

Sheriff John Ramos looked up. "Howdy, stranger."

"Evening, Sheriff." Blackie surveyed the office.

"What can I do for you?"

Blackie started to reply, but stopped when he saw Jessica's trunk in a corner of the room. He walked toward it.

"Hey, where you going?"

"This looks like my sister's trunk. Jessica Raymond. Is she still here?"

"No. She left about three weeks ago." The sheriff eyed him closely.

Blackie tried the lid. "It's locked."

"She took the key with her." The sheriff rose from his desk.

"Do you know where she went?"

"She went to California with a man named Jake Harwood."

"Thank you, Sheriff." Blackie tipped his hat and walked out the door.

The sheriff scratched his head. *Didn't look much like his sister.*

Blackie headed for the livery stable, then the hotel.

* * * *

Maco, the tall young Apache felt the missed gait as his pinto struggled to keep pace with the rest of the raiders. *Stealing the white man's horses was one of his greatest pleasures.* He dropped farther back from the pack as they neared the deep arroyo, but still urged his fatigued mount. Apache custom was to run a horse to death, then eat it for food.

The war party started through the riverbed not noticing Maco had fallen behind. They galloped around a bend when Maco's horse threw him. The animal stumbled after catching its right front hoof in a hole. Dazed, Maco examined his torn leather leggings, then pulled off the war band that held his long, black hair and wrapped it around his bloody leg. He lifted upright with his lance. His pony had broken its right foreleg. He withdrew his rifle from its sheath and sent a bullet through the pony's brain. Taking his rifle and lance with him, Maco limped across the next group of rocks toward the Apache stronghold, located several miles away in one of the desolate canyons that cracked the spacious desert.

When he neared another dry wash, he heard the sound of approaching horses. He crouched behind several large rocks with the sun at his back. A man and woman rode over the crest of the hill that led to the gully. Maco, paint across his eyes, waited.

Jake and Jessica had risen early that morning and after a quick breakfast started out, pushing their horses hard all morning and early afternoon. They ambled down the steep embankment to the dry gulch.

"We better rest the horses here." Jake motioned to Jessica.

"Good idea. I could use a little rest, too." She drew a hand across her forehead.

He dismounted, slapped the dust off his pants with his hat, then wiped his brow. "It's pretty warm."

Jessica dismounted also and poured some water from her canteen on her bandanna. "Aaaah, this is refreshing." She patted her face with the cool cloth.

Jake scanned the maze of rocks that lined the crevice. Shadows from the afternoon sunlight slithered from boulder to boulder, sometimes altering the colors. He examined the tracks in the sand. "Unshod ponies came through here."

Jessica leaned over for a closer look. "How long ago?"

"Less than an hour."

"Do you think they were Apaches?"

"Yes, but a couple of the hoof prints were from shod horses, probably stolen. We better get going."

As they approached their mounts, they did not see the pair of black eyes watching them from the other side of the wash. Maco picked up his war lance and pressed it close to his body.

Jake started to mount his horse when the lance sailed through the air and pierced his right shoulder. "Jessica, get down!"

The Apache stepped from behind a rock and leveled his rifle at the pair. Jake, blood streaming down his right arm, tried to draw his weapon, but his gun hand would not respond. The warrior shook his head and penetrated Jake's eyes with his. After a few moments of the stare-down, Jake's arm went limp.

Jessica, still crouched on the ground and stunned, felt the force between the two men, but did not move. The brave motioned with his rifle for Jake and her to remain still as he approached. Then he mounted Jake's buckskin and pointed for Jessica to get up behind him.

"No!" She rose, pulled off her wet bandanna, and made a sling for Jake's arm.

Maco waved his rifle at Jake to mount Jessica's pinto. Then he pulled Jessica behind him and set out along the riverbed at a fast trot.

After an hour's ride through sand and rock, the Apache stopped the horses next to a small waterhole. When the horses had their fill of water, Maco backtracked a few miles to the entrance of a small canyon. The trail led to the encampment of twenty or so Apaches, the main band of raiders. His fellow warriors greeted Maco with whoops and hollers. Maco bragged about his prisoners after relating his story. He ordered Jessica held at their campfire and Jake staked face-up to the ground near a rocky ledge.

* * * *

After his talk with Sheriff Ramos the night before, Blackie Le Font left Adobe Crossing early the next morning, refreshed from a good night's sleep. Ace, his big black stallion, won long ago in a poker game, thundered over the trail with the grace and ease of a thoroughbred. *Gambling was his way of life* . . . .

André, Blackie's real name, had moved to New Orleans with his family at the age of ten. Jean Le Font, his father, was master of a large shipping empire in France, but sought the New World and settled in the Louisiana seaport. He now traded mostly in the West Indies.

André worked on the ships doing whatever was needed. He became an expert seaman and diligently watched the other sailors gamble in their spare time. The excitement of winning and losing fascinated him; he decided cards were a better way to make a living than seamanship.

When André was nineteen, cargo pirates killed his father. Two years later, his mother died. André sold all the ships and opened a gambling hall. He had a knack for coming up with the Ace of Spades in five-card stud games and spade flushes in draw poker. His Blackjacks in 21 always seemed to be spades. Soon the other gamblers started calling him Blackie.

He liked the name and began wearing black. A black string tie hung loosely in a bow on his ruffled white shirt. His tailored black broadcloth pants fitted closely on his wiry six-foot-two frame. A black velvet vest fitted snugly under his short black frock coat. His black boots never lacked a shine and under his left shoulder he wore a holster containing a small revolver. In his gunbelt rode a Colt .44 with black pearl handles. He never went out without his black walking stick topped with a shiny gold knob.

Blackie's reputation as an honest gambler grew and Blackie's Saloon and Gambling Hall thrived. Not many men messed with him. . . .

Four days after leaving Adobe Crossing, Blackie entered the canyons of the Chiricahua Apaches. He had no experience against hostile Indians, but instincts that had helped him out of many tight spots before made him proceed with caution.

Blackie kept his eyes peeled toward the tops of the canyons as he made his way west. Shadows filtered into the gullies and gulches hiding potential danger. He scanned each side of the narrow crevices, then slowed Ace's gait to a walk when he saw the hoofprints of two horses in the sand. After a few strides, he stopped, checked his pistol, then continued. The trail seemed to vanish into the rocks, but after closer inspection Blackie saw it worked its way around a large collection of rounded boulders and went up the side of the canyon. Hearing nothing but the wind, he pulled his gun and proceeded slowly.

CHAPTER SIX

Strapped down to a three-legged stand of tree branches, Jessica Raymond struggled against the rawhide. Fire crackled beneath a cooking pot and gave off dancing shadows on the rocky ledge above Jake Harwood, spread-eagled in the soft earth.

Maco, the Apache leader, walked around, inspected the camp, and gazed at the fading sun. He felt hunger pangs inside his tight stomach, then motioned to Jessica to prepare the evening meal.

She tugged on her bonds, glared at the rugged warrior. "I can't."

Maco loosened the restraints on her outstretched legs and hands.

"Thank you." She sat up, brushed her dirty riding pants, and rubbed her wrists.

He surveyed her as she slowly stood, but said nothing. *She was not Apache, but a fine looking woman. He'd never had a white woman, but felt her bounce against his back when they rode together. Her eyes blazed at him, but what did she think?*

After their food, several of the braves argued among themselves to see who would take Jessica. She cringed, sank next to the tripod, and stared into the flames. Her arms and legs trembled until she pressed her hands on her arms.

Maco, after checking on the picketed horses, walked toward the fighting warriors. They stopped brawling when they saw him and backed away. He gestured to Jessica that she would go with him in the morning. He threw her a blanket. His eyes told her not to resist.

She wrapped the blanket around her shoulders and drew her knees up close.

Would he take her for himself? He was crudely handsome for an Apache. She'd never seen one close up before. He was almost as tall as Jake. What would she do if he wanted her?

Jake, still tied to the stakes, watched and listened to the Apaches' treatment of Jessica. *If he was killed or left behind, she'd have to survive on her own. He couldn't help her.* Darkness closed around him and after one more struggle to get free, he drifted into a restless sleep.

First light came and brought forth overcast gray skies. The raiding party prepared for the journey to their mountain fortress. The campfire's red embers were scuffed out and scattered by a young brave who also untied the horses.

Maco cut Jessica loose and set her on Jake's buckskin. She looked to see if Jake was freed also, but Maco waved her off. One of the braves tied a rawhide strip around Jake's throat and poured water over it.

Jessica watched in horror, knowing that when the sun came out later in the day, the leather band's constriction would siphon Jake's life away. The cry in her throat would not come out.

Jake tried to watch as the Apache raiders and Jessica rode out of sight, but could see only the cloud-covered sky above him. *Thank God the sun wasn't searing him yet.* Thunder rumbled in the distance. *He didn't need a cloudburst rushing down the arroyo.* The more he struggled with the rawhide strips around his wrists and feet, the more his throat ached from the pull around his neck. Then he heard the sound of hooves against stones. He stiffened. *Were the Apaches coming back to finish him?* He struggled with his bonds, but the rawhide did not give. He tensed, waited.

Blackie eased Ace around the curve next to the ledge Jake was under. He saw Jake lying face-up, leaped from his horse, and rushed to the large man pinned to the ground.

"Apaches?" Blackie bent down.

"Yeah." Jake relaxed.

Blackie pulled a knife from his belt, cut him free.

Jake rubbed his wrists, sat up slowly, and cut the rawhide from around his throat. "That's better." He took several breaths.

Blackie took the canteen from his saddle, offered it to Jake.

He gulped the water down, spilling some down his front. "I need your help, Stranger."

"Sure, if I can."

"A Chiricahua raiding party took a friend, a woman, to their mountain camp."

"A woman? I'm afraid she's out of luck."

"I know, but I have to try and get her back."

"I'll help, but it's probably futile."

"All right, let's go. I'm Jake Harwood."

"Blackie Le Font." He held out a hand. *The sheriff said Jessica went with him.*

Jake drew back. *So this was Jessica's Blackie. Big surprise—but he needed him now.* Then he shook Blackie's hand. "Can your horse carry both of us?"

"Easy. Ace here is a great stallion."

"Then let's get going."

Blackie reached into his saddlebag. "First we better eat something."

"Good idea. We can pick up their trail on the other side of the rocks."

* * * *

Maco rode behind Jessica. *She carried herself well—didn't seem afraid. Rode like an Indian. He'd have to weigh what to do with her.*

When they came out of the canyon Maco signaled and they turned in a westerly direction toward the mountains beyond a purple and bronze mesa.

Jessica turned back to Maco. *It would be nightfall before they reached camp. Would he keep her close to him tonight? Strangely, she was not afraid of him. He could have killed her by now had he wished. Did he want her for his own? He wasn't like any of the other men she'd dealt with during her twenty-eight years. She saw the pride and strength in him as he rode her pinto. She was confused, didn't understand the strong feeling of warmth that slowly flooded her body.* She turned forward again.

Maco rode silently. *Why did this beautiful woman turn and look at him? What was she thinking? Would the coming darkness make her tighten with fear or panic? He didn't understand his strange feelings about her. Why he wished to court her as an Indian maid. A warrior should take his prey, especially a white woman.*

* * * *

The sun faded into a shading dusk as Jake and Blackie galloped toward the high mesa.

Jake glanced at the sky, then to the distant mountains. "They won't make it to the stronghold before dark."

"We'll never see their trail after nightfall," Blackie said.

"Won't need to. Their campfire will show up for miles in this clear sky."

* * * *

Maco halted the raiders for the night at a spot below a high plateau where sand and cliff melded together. They picketed their horses on the outer perimeter and started a fire. Maco dismounted first then motioned Jessica to get off her horse and start cooking cornmeal in a pot.

After the raiding party had their fill of food, they kept the fire going strong to ward off stray coyotes. Maco did not bind Jessica, but positioned her on a blanket close to him. She lay still not knowing what to expect. He threw down another blanket, crawled on it, and turned his back to her.

* * * *

Jake was the first to see the flickering brightness against the high walls of sandstone. He nudged Blackie who slowed his large horse to a trot.

"We'll come in from the northeast," Jake said.

Blackie understood; the wind was coming from the southwest. They staked Ace a half mile away and started toward the light, Jake with a rifle and Blackie with his revolver. The Indian ponies moved slightly back and forth from their stakes as the two men crept between them. When Jake found his horse, Sam, he stroked the buckskin's back with a quieting motion. As they drew near the camp, only one of the ponies let out a slight whimper which did not stir the war party.

"We're in luck," Jake whispered. "There's no guard."

Blackie signaled back. "Yeah, luck."

The braves slept soundly scattered in various positions around the campfire. Jessica, lying by a sandstone boulder near Maco, stirred slightly. *He hadn't touched her, but she sensed his masculine closeness. Survival was her key. She'd do anything to stay alive. He was savagely handsome, but she couldn't think about that. Would his animal instincts take her?*

Maco, deep in sleep, jerked as Jake's large hand covered his mouth. He pushed the cutting steel of his knife against Maco's throat. Maco's eyes flashed open; he stared into Jake's dilated pupils, chose against a struggle.

At the same instant, Blackie's hand muffled Jessica's cry of amazement as she recognized him. Blackie saw who she was, restrained his emotions, and held his hand tight against her mouth.

By this time, Jake had his bandanna around Maco's mouth and tied his hands behind his back with a strip of rawhide reata. Jake pulled the warrior's hunting knife from its sheath and stuck it into the ground. *He should kill him, but he had a certain respect for the young Apache. They would meet again.*

Jake, Jessica, and Blackie crawled back to the picketed horses, untied Sam and the pinto, and led them toward Blackie's stallion.

Jessica turned to Blackie. "I thought you were dead."

31

"No thanks to you, I'm not." He glared at her.
Jake motioned to them. "Let's get out of here."

CHAPTER SEVEN

The large black and white pinto halted behind a cluster of willows near the edge of a small pond on a late summer afternoon. A young warrior eased off his horse's back and crept toward the sound of splashing water.

Named for Geromino's grandfather, he felt the pride of his name, Maco. He was Chiricahua Apache. He was enemy. Taller than most, Maco stood more than six feet tall, with broad shoulders covered by a blue soldier coat tightly fitted on his hard frame.

The splashing grew louder. Maco crept closer to the water and adjusted his war lance in his rough hands. He felt the wet earth through his leather moccasins and remembered when the ground was not so soft beneath his feet. To become a man, he had been forced to survive in the desert and mountains for two full moons with nothing but his own brute strength and cunning. Using the knowledge and instructions given him as a child by his parents, he mastered the first test required of him.

Maco, not yet a chief, knew his time was soon. The other braves admired him when he won wrestling matches or finished first in the water and foot races. He could run more than five miles holding a mouthful of water without spilling or swallowing any. In his wickiup, Maco hoisted the most scalps from the hated Comanches and Mexicans, who put a bounty on Apache scalps. It was pleasure and custom for the Apache to steal horses; Maco enjoyed more pleasure than any other warrior.

At the water's edge now, Maco crouched and parted the tall reeds with his thick fingers. His wide, deep-set black eyes, with a constant determined look, relaxed when he saw the slender young Indian woman. She stood under a gentle waterfall, across the shallow pond, spraying cool water on her small breasts. Her dark-brown nipples stood straight out; for a long time Maco watched her play in the water. His nostrils, flaring like a giant stallion whenever danger threatened, breathed in a different manner now. He had never felt such a sensation before and savored the sight of the bronze beauty glistening in the water.

The girl turned. Maco raised his head. Seeing him, she dropped her arms, covered herself. Maco made no move. She stood still, staring at the Apache brave with long, straight black hair hanging loose on his shoulders. A wide strip of white paint spread across his broad nose and hard cheekbones made him look even more ferocious. She knew his tight lips, above his full square jaw, would never open to pain.

Maco adjusted the buckskin war band on his weathered forehead and started toward her. The maiden never moved, but followed his penetrating eyes as they toured her every feature. She let out a short breath when he stopped after a few steps, realizing his inspection of her seemed to please him. Then she walked through the water and gathered her clothes on the bank.

Maco stared. *She must be Cheyenne.*

She then put on a Comanche dress.

He looked around the pond. *Would a young Comanche warrior come seeking his woman?* Maco motioned with his lance and she obeyed his silent command to go with him. He mounted the big pinto first and the girl climbed on behind him. As they trotted away from the pool, he felt her warm body against his back. Her hands tugged at his waist and her feet held tight against his leather leggings. Eyes straight ahead, ears alert, new sensations flashed through his mind. *This woman would be Apache.*

* * * *

The copper-skinned young woman reined her spotted pony and dismounted behind a group of tall cottonwoods. A warm summer breeze fluttered through the branches as she pulled off her wet beaded headband and unbraided her hair. She walked quickly down the narrow pathway to her secret pond as she had many times before. At the pool's edge, she sat on a rock and stared into the water. Captured by the Comanches ten years ago, she had never forgotten her parents . . . .

Her father, a burly French trapper, had helped build Bent's Trading Fort in Cheyenne Country. Her mother, a Southern Cheyenne maiden, had picked the jovial white man over the childish youths of her tribe.

"My older brother must name the newborn," his wife, lying under thick hides with their first child, told her husband.

"No," the trapper said, "my baby girl will be named Susan, after my mother." He backed out of the tipi, raised his massive frame, and fired his great rifle into the air several times, hitting a low-flying hawk.

The tribe's elders, surprised by this outburst, thought it a good omen and named the baby, Blackhawk.

"Susan Blackhawk!" The trapper danced in a circle. "I like that!"

The Cheyenne did not tolerate crying babies, so Susan nursed on her mother's milk as much as needed. Sometimes her father held her close to his chest so she learned he was not a woman.

For nine years the little girl lived the Cheyenne way of life, learning what chores were expected of her. She spent many hours listening to captivating stories from the elders.

"More important," her mother stressed, "be chaste, be honest, be generous—then life will fall in place."

Susan's short leisure time was spent playing house with leather tipis and with dolls made from stuffed deerskin.

One day, while her father was away trapping, Susan and her mother dug for roots and gathered wood for their fire. When they returned to camp, a Comanche raiding party ravaged the village.

"Run! Hide!" Her mother pushed Susan toward the trees and ran the opposite way.

A Comanche warrior spotted them and rode Susan's mother down. She put up a fight, but the brave threw his lance into her chest. Susan ran to her mother's side and held her head in her lap as her mother took her last breath. The Comanche jabbed his lance at Susan until she was herded along with the other captives and fine Cheyenne horses.

Each day of captivity, Susan Blackhawk waited for her father to lead a raid on the Comanches and rescue her. As the months and years passed, he never came. Eventually, she learned from a hunter, friendly with the Comanches, that he had been killed by a grizzly. So, she resigned herself to life with her enemies. But, she knew she would always be Cheyenne. Growing into her teens, she remembered her mother's words—be chaste, be honest, be generous. She had not exchanged glances, smiles, or many conversations with the young Comanche braves and had kept her chastity hide tight around her slim waist and thighs . . . .

The sun inched past the high spot in the cloudless sky as Susan Blackhawk shed her long buckskin dress and stepped into the cool, shallow pond. She walked toward the water gently cascading from a high, rocky incline. Her long, black hair shone as the first drops of water touched it. Raising her intense, dark eyes to the soothing fountain, she pulled her hair back and relaxed a moment. Then she massaged the water across her round cheeks and down her neck past the tiny shell necklace her father had given her. Soon, she splashed and sprayed water over her entire figure. Her tall body, inherited from her father, was firm and supple from years of gathering wood, digging prairie turnips, hiding buffalo, and playing outdoors in summer and winter.

Savoring the pleasant feeling of water misting on her small breasts, making her dark nipples rigid, Susan sensed another person's closeness. Parting her lips, she lifted her nose into the air away from the falling water. Taking a few sniffs, no unknown scents came to her. All she heard was water hitting the pool and rippling outward in curved patterns. The sun's hot rays bounced off her smooth upper body. The heat felt good against her wet skin. Thinking her senses had played tricks; Susan continued her bath under the lightly falling shower.

It was not until he parted the tall reeds on the other side of the pond and stood up, that she saw the tall Apache warrior. She gasped and dropped her hands to cover herself. He started toward her. She held her ground, but followed his penetrating eyes searching her every part. *Maybe it had been the water arousing her. Maybe it was his eyes, but somehow sensations she had never known shot through her in those few tense moments. His inspection of her seemed to please him.*

With a guarded smile, Susan Blackhawk waited as he approached. Stopping, he motioned with his war lance. She started to speak, but the gasp that came out was just above a whisper.

CHAPTER EIGHT

The long hard ride back to Adobe Crossing was tiring for Jessica. She kept watching Blackie riding in front with Jake. *What happened at his hotel after it went up in flames? How did he survive? He should've been killed. How did he find Jake? He did save him, though. The hate she felt for him dissipated some. After all, he did risk his life for her now.* Her pinto's pounding hooves on the stage trail that led into Adobe Crossing interrupted her thoughts. The morning sun peeked its bold, flaming face over the flat desert horizon. Jessica blinked into the glare.

The three riders spurred their great horses at a faster pace toward the sleeping village that knew nothing of their ordeal. Every once in a while, Jake rubbed his right shoulder where Maco's lance had pierced it. His arm still felt numb, but he weathered the pain.

The dust stirred ever so slightly as the trio walked their tired horses down the main street of the quiet town not yet awake. They reined up in front of the sheriff's office and walked in.

Sheriff Ramos looked up from his desk. "Well I'll be . . . didn't think I'd see any of you again."

"It was close," Jake said. "We had a little run-in with the Apaches."

After Jake told him their story, the sheriff sat back, put his hands behind his head. "You're lucky you made it here. Funny though, this town has never been attacked by the Apaches since I've been here."

"That's good, but I'd be on the alert." Jake turned. "We'll be at the hotel."

Jessica watched Blackie intensely as they crossed the street, now beginning to stir with the weekday commerce. At the hotel, they decided to catch some sleep before talking things over. Jessica lay on the bed in her small room; Blackie moved through her thoughts until a deep sleep overtook her. Jake, exhausted, fell asleep as soon as he hit the pillow. Blackie put his gunbelt on the table next to his bed, climbed into it, and drifted into a restless sleep.

Morning came swiftly to the weary adventurers who had slept straight through the rest of that day and until daylight streaked in.

Blackie awoke first, went down to the dining room, and ordered coffee. *Jessica had aroused a great deal of anger in him back in New Orleans, but somehow it didn't matter as much now. For the first time in his life, he'd helped someone in distress. A feeling of satisfaction coursed through him.*

Jessica and Jake walked down the stairs together and entered the dining room. Blackie drank his second cup of coffee, looked up. "Morning."

"Mornin'." Jake nodded.

"Hello." Jessica's smile disappeared. *She and Blackie had unfinished business.*

Jake and Jessica ordered coffee, ham, and eggs from the stout waitress. Blackie ordered flapjacks and eggs.

"Sure glad you happened along that canyon when you did." Jake slapped Blackie on the shoulder.

"Yeah, we had quite a time, but it's worked out okay." He smiled, but his eyes lingered on Jessica.

She raised her eyebrows at his gaze. "I didn't expect to see you again."

"I know." He turned from her when his food came.

Not much else was said after the food was served.

Jessica kept Blackie in the corner of her eye. *When the time was right, she'd have to talk to him privately.*

Jake finished first. "I'll go check on the horses. Meet you both here later." He got up, walked out the front door.

They watched him leave, then turned to each other.

"I don't know what to say, Blackie," Jessica said. "In New Orleans, I really hated you. Father meant so much to me. When I lost him, I blamed you."

Blackie leaned forward, folded his hands. "Arthur cheated at cards. I couldn't let that pass. My integrity was at stake. No gambler would ever again sit at my tables. Besides, he drew for his gun. I thought you knew how sorry I was at the funeral."

"I thought you were gloating." Her eyes moistened. "Later I saw a chance for revenge, when you wanted me at your hotel."

He half-smiled. "The offer of work was legitimate, but I admit I was attracted to you."

She softened. "I'm glad you're alive. Not only for saving Jake and me, but I've changed my mind about you somewhat."

"Well, what now? I've nothing left in New Orleans."

"Me either." She raised her eyes to his.

"You know, when I rode through here the first time looking for you, I thought this town would be a natural stop between Santa Fe and Tucson."

Jessica tilted her head. "I don't understand."

"Well, it seems to me that this old hotel could use a little dressing up. Maybe the owner would be interested in doing some business."

"You mean you want to buy this place?"

"Yes, and I'd consider a partner, specially one who has some of my money."

"I was going to tell you about that." She pulled back.

"That's all right—for now. The past is done."

Jake Harwood walked through the front door at that moment. "The horses are fed and rested. Guess I'll head out tomorrow. Those gold fields won't last forever." He turned for Jessica. "You still going?"

"I don't know, Jake. Blackie wants to buy this hotel and needs a partner. Who knows, someday this could be a booming city."

"It could be a good investment," Blackie said. "You interested?"

Jake stood tall. "No, that's not for me. Don't want to be tied down again."

"Then I guess I'll take him up on the offer." Jessica leaned back in her chair.

Blackie smiled, extended his hand to her. "Partner."

"This calls for a celebration tonight." Jake hid his letdown. *He'd hoped she would go west with him.*

CHAPTER NINE

The sun blazed down from straight above as a lone rider walked his large sorrel horse into town at the far end of Adobe Crossing. Glen Calhoun, known as Lefty on wanted posters, needed a change of horse. He stopped in front of the Trail Saloon and dismounted slowly. Scanning both sides of the street, he tied his weary horse to a post. *Surely no wanted posters would have circulated this far south. Dodge City was a long way off.* His dark-green, heavy pants and striped white shirt were barely visible under the coat of trail dust that covered them. He hit his legs with a few powerful lashes of his soiled hat and adjusted his gunbelt on his left side. His gun had no notches, but had the worn look it should contain several. A quick glance left and right assured him his Winchester would be safe in the saddle sheath. Then he started up the saloon's steps.

Wind and sun had darkened Lefty's face, but little Johnny Woods, standing by the saloon's corner, recognized him anyway as the outlaw pushed through the saloon's swinging doors.

Johnny did odd jobs for the sheriff and postmaster after school and on Saturdays. He was fascinated by wanted posters. Studying the mean-looking desperados on paper was one way of fulfilling his dreams of someday becoming a marshal. The sheriff played along with him.

Johnny turned, ran to the sheriff's office. "Sheriff, Sheriff— I saw him! I saw him!"

Sheriff Ramos looked up from his desk. "Calm down, Johnny. Saw who?"

"The man in this stack of posters that came in last week." He dug through the papers until he found Lefty Calhoun's face pasted under 'Wanted'. "It says here, he murdered a marshal in Dodge."

Sheriff Ramos rose. "Johnny, you stay here." He checked the cartridges in his six-shooter, then walked to the wall where two rifles and a shotgun hung. Hesitating a moment, he chose the shotgun and loaded his vest pockets with shells from his desk drawer.

Adobe Crossing had no deputy, so the old lawman stood alone whenever trouble arose.

Inside the saloon, Glen Calhoun sat at a side table near the front doors. When he ordered his whiskey, he inquired about a nearby room and the whereabouts of the livery stable. Lefty's brutal seriousness got him immediate directions to both.

After slugging down his shot of whiskey, Calhoun caught the sheriff pushing through the swinging doors. He looked the sheriff square in the eyes.

"Let's go Lefty." Sheriff Ramos pivoted his shotgun into a threatening position.

The crafty outlaw froze. *He'd seen a man's head shot off with a scattergun once and wanted no part of it. He'd bide his time.*

Without warning, Jim Hughes, the town drunk, stumbled through the doors. It was time for his morning shot of rye. The swinging door on the right side hit the sheriff's left elbow just enough to jar him. Lefty made his move. He shoved the table away with his right hand and dropped his lightning-quick left hand to his six-gun. Bullets burst out with each squeezed-off round from his trigger finger. The old sheriff reacted too slowly.

Three slugs cut through his chest. He lunged backward, hit the floor hard.

The other men in the room cowered under tables, chairs, and in corners. Calhoun whirled around, backed toward the closest wall.

Johnny peeked his head around the corner of the front window just as the lawman fell. His eyes seemed to jump out of his head. He turned, ran to the hotel.

Jake heard the gunfire from the hotel steps as Johnny came running.

"Mister, Mister! Come quick! The sheriff's been shot!"

Jake tugged at his gunbelt, felt the handle of his Colt .44, and started across the street with Johnny. He kept his right hand on his gun. *The last time he'd used his gun was in Wichita, against the stream of raw gunslingers who threatened to take over the town.*

Calhoun backed out of the saloon, but turned toward the street when he heard Jake and Johnny. Jake pushed Johnny away when he saw Lefty's pistol swing around. Jake dodged to his right as Calhoun shot. His own gun cleared its holster by the time he steadied himself. Lefty fell off the boardwalk when Jake's bullet tore through the badman's throat. Jake waited . . .

Johnny picked himself up from the dusty street. "Wow!"

Calhoun quivered once before life passed from him. Jake headed toward him with his Colt cocked again.

Persons from the other businesses and buildings strode into the street before anyone emerged from the Trail Saloon. The morning patrons of the bar stood silent, still stunned by the horror of what had just occurred.

"What do we do?" one of the numbed citizens asked.

"Somebody get the undertaker," another said.

Blackie and Jessica rushed from the hotel to where Jake stood in front of the saloon.

"You okay?" Blackie tapped Jake's shoulder.

"Yeah." He held his gun with quiet confidence.

Jessica, wide-eyed, stared at Calhoun's body, then at Jake. "Are you sure you're all right?"

"I'm fine." He holstered his gun.

The street filled with the rest of the townspeople, including the mayor and town council members.

"That was some shooting," the mayor said.

"Darn tootin'," one of the council members replied.

"He didn't have to shoot the sheriff." Jake turned toward the saloon. "Is he still alive?"

The mayor stepped forward. "No, he's gone. Sheriff Ramos was a good man. It'll be hard to replace him."

"Here's your man, Mayor." The council member pointed to Jake.

"Yes, why not? What do you say, young man?"

Jake backed up. "Sorry Mayor, but I'm leaving for California tomorrow."

"Hold on, mister. This town needs a good sheriff. There's law-biding citizens here who need protection from outlaws. We're growing and the railroad is thinking of passing through here."

"Like I said, Mayor—I'm moving on."

"You could make a good living here. We would pay you well."

Jessica moved closer to Jake. "Jake, take the job, please."

He looked at her pleading eyes. "Mind's made up. Had my fill of marshaling."

"I don't blame you, Jake," Blackie said. "Still, you're mighty handy with that gun."

Jake looked him square in the eyes. "Only when it's necessary."

The mayor saw the determination on Jake's face. He turned to the other council members. "It's no use. We'll have to send word to Santa Fe."

Jake tipped his hat, started down the boardwalk toward the General Store. *He'd better outfit himself for the long journey tomorrow.*

Four miles out of town, off the main road, Pete Thatcher, hard-faced and lean, sat waiting under an organ-pipe cactus. Lefty Calhoun had told him if everything went well, he would be back with the horses by early afternoon.

By the sun, it neared three o'clock; Pete paced back and forth, kept gazing down the dusty road. *He'd give Lefty a while longer, then go into town.* He gripped the Henry lever-action rifle tighter, wedged the stock deeper into the sand.

CHAPTER TEN

Susan Blackhawk clung tighter to Maco's ribs when she saw the sentries at the entrance to the tribe's encampment. Maco waved. The sentries thrust their rifles in the air. Maco spurred his horse into camp. The Indian women and old men glanced up from their chores as the riders passed. The young braves stared long and hard at Susan's beauty, but turned away when Maco caught their eye. He was leader. He had his choice of women.

Maco stopped at his wickiup, dismounted, and offered to help Susan off his paint. At first she hesitated, but then took his hand as he lifted her to the ground. *This was strange to her. The Comanche had not been so gentle. What sort of man was this Apache?*

He motioned for her to enter the wickiup, but did not follow. Inside, the hut smelled smoky from the buffalo dung burning in the fire pit in the middle of the room. She spotted his lances and shields against a wall and several scalps hung from a staff. A rifle and war knife was stashed in another area. A bedroll, half rolled up lay near the fire pit. Nothing that indicated a woman was present in the wickiup.

Maco conferred with the other warriors, told them how he came across the beautiful captive, part white and Cheyenne.

"The Cheyenne are enemies." One brave stepped forward.

Maco turned to him with cold eyes. "This woman is not enemy. She will be Apache."

The warrior hesitated a moment, then retreated.

"That is settled," Maco said. "Tomorrow we raid the stage. There is gold aboard. It will buy back our people from the Mexicans."

"Why not just raid the Mexicans?" another brave asked.

Maco looked at him sharply. "Our number is small. We need more strength."

The afternoon sun sank lower in the sky as the meeting adjourned. Maco waved the others away, walked across the camp to his lodge. He pulled back the deerskin covering the opening and bent his head when he entered.

Susan Blackhawk looked up and stepped back when she saw Maco's imposing figure. He motioned to the fire pit and the mesquite wood beside the buffalo chips. She understood he wanted the wood thrown into the fire.

After the fire roared up, Maco pulled a fur close to it and sat down. He motioned for her to join him. Susan waited a moment, then sat beside him. He smiled at her, which surprised her and they watched the sparks ascend upward in silence.

Soon, an old woman opened the flap and told Maco the food was ready. Susan followed him outside.

After supper of corn tortillas and beans, Susan started to join the other women, but Maco stopped her and motioned her to his wickiup. He did not follow her immediately, instead had a smoke with the old men and other warriors.

Susan sat on the fur beside the fire when Maco walked into the lodge. She brushed her long black hair with her fingers and stared into his penetrating eyes. He stopped, watched her, then sat next to her. She trembled at his presence, but tried not to show it. Maco felt her tentativeness, turned away, and let a small smile cross his lips.

After awhile, his eyes grew heavy and he moved to the bedroll. Susan did not move. *She did not know what to do. Was she supposed to bed with him or stay by the fire? The Comanche had let her be because she fought them fiercely each time a chief went after her. She was known as 'Woman Who Fights'. At least she retained her virginity until now. Would this great Apache take her by force or would he try to seduce her?* She stared at his bare chest half-covered in the bedroll and sensed his animal magnetism.

Maco awakened at first light, saw his captive still asleep on the fur. *It was good he did not take her. There was plenty of time.*

The wickiup's front flap opened. An old woman peeked in, pointed to the sleeping captive. "She must help with the early-day chores."

Maco waved, shook Susan's shoulder. She stirred, wiped her eyes, and tugged at her hair. He motioned for her to rise and go with the old woman. He then rose, stretched, and grabbed his knife. The other warriors waited for him outside at the council fire.

CHAPTER ELEVEN

The afternoon sun started its descent toward the horizon when Pete Thatcher decided to go into town. *Lefty was long overdue and he needed to know what happened.* Pete adjusted his gunbelt and shoved the Henry rifle into its sheath next to three Apache scalps on his horse's saddle.

In Adobe Crossing, Pete reined up at the saloon and inquired about his partner, Lefty. He was told the tall stranger had killed a left-handed gunman after the sheriff had been shot down.

"Where can I find this stranger?" Pete asked the bartender.

"He's probably still at the hotel."

Pete walked out of the saloon, pulled the Henry out of the saddle sheath, and headed for the hotel.

Jake came out of the hotel, stood beside a pillar on the front porch, and eyed the hard-faced gunman walking toward him. Pete gripped the Henry rifle tighter in his right hand and looked Jake square in the eyes. Jake moved away from the post, adjusted his gunbelt, and stood tall, feet spread apart. Pete hoisted his rifle level with his waist and pointed it at Jake. His finger brushed the trigger. Jake saw the movement, dropped his hands to his sides just as Pete pulled the trigger of the Henry. The bullet shot past Jake's left ear. He slapped the handle of his .44 and drew it faster than a cobra's strike. Fire blazed out of the barrel and the bullet tore into Pete's right shoulder. He doubled up in pain and dropped his rifle. Jake shot off another round into Pete's chest; Pete crashed to the dirt face down. Jake turned, started back to the hotel. Pete stirred, reached for his rifle, and put a slug into Jake's upper back by his left shoulder blade. He grabbed his bloody shoulder, fell hard to the ground. Pete lowered his rifle. He slumped on it and lay still.

Hearing the gunfire, Jessica and Blackie bolted out of the hotel. They saw the fallen Jake and ran toward him.

"Oh, my God!" Jessica bent down, put her ear to his chest.

Blackie raised Jake's head, looked into his eyes. "Jake, look at me. Open your eyes."

Jake moaned, but his eyes remained shut.

Blackie turned toward the hotel. "Somebody get the doctor!"

Johnny Woods stood watching by the hotel's front entrance. He heard Blackie and dashed toward the doctor's office.

Jessica put pressure on Jake's shoulder to try to stop the bleeding, but the blood kept pouring out.

"Here, let me do it." Blackie ripped off his shirt, covered the wound with it while pressing down hard.

Jessica moved over. "I think you got it."

Just then, the doctor arrived with Johnny.

"Good work, Johnny." Blackie let up on the pressure.

The doctor examined Jake's shoulder. "This man's lucky, but I don't want to move him just yet. Keep more pressure on it." He dug into his bag, pulled out a scalpel. "I'm gonna dig that slug out of him right here—while he's still out."

"It looks like most of the bleeding has stopped." Blackie lifted his shirt from the wound.

After probing for the bullet, the doctor took his forceps and extracted the slug. He then bandaged Jake's arm and shoulder.

Jake opened his eyes, cringed, and raised his head. "Must be getting old—thought my first shot got him good."

"Is he going to be all right?" Jessica asked.

The doctor squinted at Jake. "He'll be fine in a few weeks."

Jake's eyes widened. "A few weeks—I'm on my way to California. I can't be laid up that long."

"Now son, you just take it easy. That's a pretty nasty wound." The doctor closed his bag.

"Listen to the Doc, Jake," Blackie said. "We'll get you going before you know it."

"Thanks, Blackie, grateful to you." Jake closed his eyes again.

"He'll be in and out of it for awhile," The doctor said.

"Yeah, we better get him to the hotel." Blackie pointed to some of the bystanders. "Here—you men—give us a hand."

Jessica followed them. "Thank God."

* * * *

Maco left the council fire satisfied he had divided up the gold from the stagecoach's strong box evenly among the war party. "There is more where that came from." He told them. "But we must pick our raids carefully."

Susan Blackhawk glanced up from her morning chores as Maco passed by. He saw her, but did not acknowledge her. Some of the other braves tracked his actions. Maco knew they were watching and did not want to show them any sign of weakness. *Inside, he reveled in her beauty.*

She in turn, gazed after him until he disappeared around a wickiup where the horses were tethered.

* * * *

Three weeks passed quickly for Jake. Jessica had changed his dressing daily and Blackie looked in on him a couple times each day.

Jake sat back on his pillow when Jessica entered his room.

"Good, you're awake." She set a tray of food on the bed stand. "Let's see if you're hungry?'

"Yeah, I'm starvin'—been awhile since I've eaten much."

"Yes, it has. You've been in and out of it for three weeks now."

"Three weeks? Has it been that long?" He raised his head. "The mountain passes will be closed if I don't get going pretty soon."

"You better concentrate on getting completely healed first."

Jake dug into his food, but had a strained look on his face.

"So, you're still bent on California." Jessica poured some coffee into his cup.

He gulped down a bite of meat. "I'm tired of gunmen comin' after me. Tired of being the man to keep law and order."

"Seems like it comes natural to you."

"Maybe so, but it gets old. Besides, there's plenty of gold to be found in California."

"I've heard that."

"You said you wanted to go west, too. What happened?" He still looked pained.

"Well, you know when Blackie offered me the hotel deal I just thought, why not?"

"I guess you forgot what he did to your father."

"No, I haven't, but he's changed. After all, he did save us from the Apaches."

"I know he did. And I like him, too." He turned away from her. "It's just that I kinda hoped you'd continue on west with me."

Jessica put a hand on his shoulder. "Jake, this isn't easy for me either. I do want to go with you, but I also feel the need to own a business, especially a hotel."

"They need hotels up in the gold country."

She turned and started for the door. "I'll think about it some more. Right now, you need to get well. I'll come up and see you later. Get some rest."

Jake stared at the door after she left. *She was right whether she went with him or not. He needed to get well. He hadn't thought much about women since Ella left, but now Jessica crossed his mind more than he wanted to admit.*

Outside in the street, a young Apache boy rode his pony toward the General Store.

He had been told not to go into Adobe Crossing by himself, but he wanted to see what they had in the white man's store. His name was Little Dog; he was twelve years old, but small and thin for his age.

Several townspeople stopped walking, turned, and stared at the young Apache guiding his pony to the hitching post in front of the General Store. Little Dog paid no attention to them. His eyes were wide open and focused on the merchandise in the front windows of the store. He dismounted and bounded up the steps. Two ladies came out of the store, saw him, and shied away. He opened the door and walked in.

The shopkeeper looked up from behind the counter. "Here, boy, what are you doing? You can't come in here."

Little Dog heard him, but kept eyeing all the goodies.

"Did you hear me, boy? I said you can't come in here."

Little Dog pointed to the candy bins, his mouth salivating.

The shopkeeper reached under the counter, pulled out a shotgun. "You better get outta here, Injun."

Little Dog's face twisted when he saw the gun pointed at him. His eyes pleaded with the man, but the man motioned him out. The boy started to turn toward the front door, then lunged for the candy. The man fired the shotgun. Buckshot tore into Little Dog's left shoulder. The force knocked him backward. He fell against a counter, blood streaming out of the wound. The man reloaded for another shot. The boy stumbled out of the shop, leaving a trail of blood. He barely climbed on his pony and headed out of town.

CHAPTER TWELVE

Jake heard the gunshot through the open window in his room. He rose from bed and looked outside. The bleeding Apache boy kicked his heels into the sides of his pony and galloped away. Jake stared after him. *What the hell was that kid doing in town and who shot him? If he dies, this town's in trouble.* He walked back to his bed and sat on the edge.

Little Dog became weaker and weaker the longer he rode. Blood poured out of his shoulder. His gaze was blurry and he slipped from side to side on his pony. Nearing the Apache stronghold, he grabbed onto the pony's mane to stay on and slumped against his horse's neck. More blood flowing from his wound, Little Dog urged his pony onward until it stopped in the middle of the camp. The boy fell off and lay motionless on the ground, face down.

Several women doing chores, stopped, screamed, and ran to him. Maco heard the commotion, peered out of his wickiup. He saw the boy lying in a pool of blood, rushed to him, and turned him over.

"Little Dog!" Maco lifted the boy to his chest, hugged him. "My brother's son, what happened to you?"

The young Apache's body was lifeless, his eyes closed, no breath emitted from him. Maco put his ear to the boy's chest, but heard no heart beat.

The women started wailing. The elders and other braves mulled around Maco and the young boy. Maco laid him on the ground and slowly rose. The wailing grew louder.

Maco raised his hands to the sky. "We will avenge this. A gunshot wound could only come from the White-Eyes."

A few days later, in Adobe Crossing, Jake Harwood rose from his bed, flexed his bad arm, and felt no pain. "It's about time. I'm getting out of here." He put on his clothes and gunbelt and walked out.

Downstairs in the dining room, he saw Jessica and Blackie sitting at a table.

Blackie looked up. "Well, here comes Jake now."

Jessica turned. "Jake—you're up. Come, join us."

"Yeah, I'm up." He sat down. "Hungry and rarin' to go."

"So, you're still bent on California." Blackie said.

"That's right. Soon as I can get outfitted." He turned to Jessica. "What about you?'

She took a big swallow of coffee and set her cup down. "I told you Jake, I think I'm staying here."

"Right—that's what you said." He blinked. "By the way, did you see the young Apache boy who was shot the other day?"

Blackie straightened up before she could answer. "No, but we heard about it. He tried to steal something from the General Store."

"He couldn't have been more than ten or twelve. Sounds like someone was pretty trigger-happy."

Jessica stared at Blackie. "You said he was a young brave."

"That's what I heard." Blackie looked away.

"I saw him ride out of town," Jake said. "He was pretty bloody and barely hanging on to his pony. If he dies, the Apache won't take kindly to it and they'll want revenge."

Jessica's eyes grew wide. "You mean they might attack the whole town?"

"That's right—and when we least expect it."

"I don't think we have to worry much about that," Blackie said. "There should be enough manpower here to take care of any raid."

Jake stiffened. "You don't know the Apache. They are fierce fighters who don't like the white man—specially when they've been betrayed."

"So, why don't you take the sheriff's job and prevent it?" Blackie asked.

"I'll be gone, that's why. Look, I don't want to see this town ravaged because of one man's stupidity."

"But, Jake," Jessica said, "would a few days delay make that much difference to you if you could save this town?"

He peered into her eyes. "I guess not, but first I'd like to find out who shot the kid and if they did it just because he was Apache."

"I told you he stole something." Blackie put his cup down hard on the table.

"Yeah, so you said."

Maco gathered his warriors around the campfire. The wailing for the young boy had stopped after the tribe buried him so the Great Spirit could take him on the Great Mustang. Little Dog's father was the first to sharpen his lance and spread war paint on his face.

He approached Maco at the fire. "Brother, I am ready."

Maco took his brother's arm. "Porico, we will ride soon. The town will be asleep when we attack before first light."

"Little Dog was my only son. He might have been chief one day. My grief is much, but I cannot again visit the crevice in the rocks where we buried him. Only Usen will know where it is and coyotes will not disturb his remains. The white man has taken my greatest treasure. He must pay in the most cruel way."

Maco saw the fire in White Horse's eyes. "Well spoken, my brother, Porico. Now, the warriors are ready. We ride."

Jake finished his breakfast and left the hotel. The hot sun baked his face as he walked to the General Store. He wiped his brow and climbed the front steps.

Inside, the shopkeeper stood behind the counter polishing a shotgun barrel. He looked up when Jake entered. "Morning, mister."

"Mornin'." Jake approached the counter. "Heard there was a little trouble in here the other day."

The man set the shotgun on the counter. "There was. A thievin' Injun stole some merchandise."

"Wasn't he just a boy?"

"I don't know. Happened real fast."

"What did he steal?"

"How come all these questions? Have you taken over the sheriff's job?"

Jake squared his shoulders, focused on the man's eyes. "I asked what he stole?"

Sweat formed on the shopkeeper's face. He fidgeted with the cloth in his hands and shifted his weight from one foot to the other. "I don't remember. We don't want Injuns in here anyway. Where did he come from?"

"I saw him ride away—all bloody. He was Apache. Do you know what Apache means? It means enemy. The Apache give no quarter. They are hostile—they strike and run. You have put this town in dire jeopardy."

CHAPTER THIRTEEN

Maco lifted his rifle into the air. The other raiders shouted and extended bows, lances, and rifles toward the dark, pre-dawn sky. Maco led them from their stronghold at a swift pace toward Adobe Crossing.

A few lamps sprinkled light throughout the town as the Apache warriors approached. Maco motioned to some of his bowmen to spread out around the perimeter of the town. When he signaled, they lit their arrows afire and launched them at the outlying buildings. Maco waved to the other braves and spurred his stallion down the main street. They sprayed bullets and fiery arrows at buildings on both sides of the street.

Jake shot out of bed as the gunshots rang out and sprang to the hotel's window. A flaming arrow broke the glass and stuck in the wall behind him. Before he turned, several more arrows hit the hotel. The fires lit up the darkness and he ducked down under the window.

Blackie burst into his room just as he pulled on his boots. "Damn! What's going on? I'm in another hotel fire."

"It's the Apaches. They're here to avenge that boy's shooting." He strapped on his gunbelt. "Let's get outta here."

They started out the door.

"Wait a minute." Jake stopped. "Where's Jessica?"

Blackie halted. "She's down the hall from me. I'll get her."

"Hurry! I'm going outside." Jake bolted down the stairs, winced when his bad shoulder hit the wall, but kept going.

The Apache raiders rode up and down the street, whooping their war cries, shooting anything that moved, and lighting more fires. Townspeople who ran outside were cut down in their tracks, as a few cracks of gray dawn streaked the sky.

Jake crashed through the hotel's front door with his gun drawn and leveled it at a warrior riding past him. Maco, surging behind, saw Jake and took a shot at him. The bullet whizzed by his head. Jake dropped to the porch floor, but kept alert. Maco rode away.

The hotel was ablaze now. Blackie and Jessica burst out the door and crouched down when they saw Jake.

"They'll burn this whole town," Jake said.

Shots rang out all around them.

"If they don't kill us first." Blackie shot back.

Jessica stayed down. "Why are they doing this?"

"Revenge," Jake said. "The boy musta been a close relative."

Just then, the gunfire stopped. The Apaches galloped out of town.

"Well, I'll be . . ." Blackie scratched his head.

Jake stood. "I think I knew one of them. He shot at me, but missed. He looked like the Apache who captured us."

"You mean he missed you on purpose?"

"I don't know, but I could have killed him when we escaped and I didn't. They have a strange code."

"Lucky for you—and us."

Jessica lifted up. "I remember him. He could have taken me, but he didn't."

"We better help put out these fires." Jake stepped off the porch.

Blackie followed. "The stables. I'll check on the horses."

"Good. Jessica, you help with the wounded." Jake holstered his gun. "I'll try to keep some order."

Maco and his band rode hard back to their stronghold. After they dismounted and tethered the horses, Maco sought out his brother White Horse. "Porico, we put fear into the white man, but did not kill enough to avenge Little Dog."

"You are right, brother, but I am not done. I will seek a small group or one family to wreak revenge when they least suspect it."

Maco put his hand on White Horse's shoulder. "It shall be done the way you say. The Apache way."

"I saw you in front of the hotel. You looked like you could kill three of the White-Eyes. What happened?"

Maco faced his brother. "I will choose another time. They were the two men and the woman I captured. When they escaped, the tall one could have killed me, but he did not. We are now even. The next time we meet, I will kill him."

White Horse nodded. "It is fair. Now, how many warriors did we lose?"

"I counted everybody. We did not lose anyone."

"Then our raid was just." White Horse headed for his wickiup.

"Yes, and there will be more raids." Maco saw Susan Blackhawk step out of his wickiup.

She smiled, but he did not smile back. Then she walked to the fire and began cooking. While stirring the beans, she kept glancing at his imposing figure. Taller than most Apaches, he stood alone in the clearing, his black eyes flashing in the advancing sunlight. His shoulder-length shiny black hair held in place with the worn war band, he watched her work.

She smiled again, but only for a moment. Her cheeks heated at what she felt. *He was the leader, the one in charge of the band. He made the decisions—when to raid, when to kill, when to hunt—when to move on. Would he take her as a wife or would he just take her for pleasure? She twinged at the thought of his touch. But it was not a painful twinge. She had fought off the Comanche braves, but did not think she wanted to fight off this Apache leader.* She peeked at him every time he was not looking, then blushed when he glanced her way.

Maco strode toward the fire and sat on a rock. He motioned to her and she brought him some mesquite beans. He ate in silence. She crouched nearby, but did not watch him eat.

* * * *

Blackie walked back from the stables in time to see the hotel collapse from the fire. Jake stood across the street beside the jail. He motioned to Blackie.

Blackie walked over. "The horses are fine."

"Good. Too bad about the hotel. What are you and Jessica gonna do now?"

"Don't know. I'll have to talk to her. What about you?"

Jake leaned against the wall. "I'm still going to California."

"Maybe we'll have to go with you. Looks like the Apaches just wanted to put a scare into this town."

"Yeah, they didn't burn everything down and kill us all. Their leader must have remembered me. He called them off. But, they are raiders. They attack, kill, and disappear before you know what hit you. Usually it's a smaller target than a whole town."

Blackie peered at the smoldering hotel. "It means they didn't get enough vengeance for the young boy who got shot."

"You're probably right. A family or small outpost will get hit before long."

"Or a small party of people heading west."

"So, you think you're going with me?"

"I'll let you know after I talk with Jessica." He headed down the street.

Jake stood away from the wall. "You do that, Blackie, but I'll not count on it."

Blackie found Jessica in a boarding house that survived the Apache onslaught and was being used as a hospital for the wounded.

Jessica looked up from a man with a bloody chest. "Blackie, we can use your help."

"All right, I'll help you, but we need to talk."

"Talk?"

"Yeah, the hotel's gone. Jake's still going to California. I told him we might go with him."

"That's a lot to talk about." She finished bandaging the man.

"I know. I was counting on that hotel for a new start."

Jessica glanced around the room. "If you help me move some the wounded—the ones who aren't critical—then we can go and talk to Jake."

"I can do that."

After they finished their work, Jessica and Blackie left the boarding house and headed for the stables.

Jake was rubbing his stallion down when they walked in. He turned. "Sam here, is ready to go. The fires scared him."

"The Apaches scared this whole town," Blackie said.

Jessica petted Sam's neck. "Good boy. I better see to my pinto."

"He's all right." Jake finished his horse. "I looked at him earlier."

Blackie glanced at another stall. "Ace is all right, too, just a little jittery."

"Then, we're all set to go," Jake said.

Jessica turned. "That's what we wanted to talk about."

"Like I said—I'm still going to California."

"With trail mates?" she asked.

"You're welcome to come."

Blackie stepped forward. "I'm for it. Nothing left here. I can see a great opportunity out west."

"I guess you're right," Jessica said.

Jake eyed them both. "We leave in the morning."

"What about supplies?" Blackie asked.

"We'll have to get by. Pick up some on the way. The store got burned out. The

shopkeeper was killed." Jake inspected his saddle.

"There should be plenty of game on the trail." Blackie moved toward his horse.

Jessica frowned. "What about the Apache?"

"Apaches are killers—raiders. We'll have to take our chances," Jake said.

CHAPTER FOURTEEN

Just after dawn, the three riders started their journey west. The day started out cloudy and chilly, but as the sun rose it dissipated the clouds and warmed the land. Jake led a horse length ahead of Jessica and Blackie. The trail was flat and sandy and they followed the tracks of the Butterfield stage.

"Where does this trail lead?" Jessica trotted up beside Jake.

"Past those mountains there in the distance, all the way to Tucson." He pointed.

She squinted, held her hand to her forehead. "I see."

"Shouldn't we head north for the gold fields?" Blackie joined them.

Jake turned. "We will—once we leave the desert. Right now we're still in Apache country. Better keep your eyes peeled."

"Right, partner. Had enough of them for a while." Blackie scanned the horizon.

Jessica felt a chill go up her back. She turned in her saddle, first to the right then to the left.

Jake saw the uneasiness on her face. "We'll be all right."

"I hope so."

They traveled without much conversation most of the day. Toward evening, they came upon a group of hills. Jake was in the lead until he stopped.

"Look, there to the right beyond that second hill." He pointed.

A sudden puff of smoke rose above the hill's crest and dissolved into the atmosphere.

"What does it mean?" Jessica reined up.

Jake strained, waited for another signal. "Means they saw us, but don't think we're too armed to harm them."

"You mean the Apaches?" she asked.

"Yeah, they've probably been following us for a spell."

Blackie withdrew his rifle from its sheath. "Think we'll need this?"

"Hope not, but we'll know soon." Jake spurred Sam to a trot. "Better find some shelter in those foothills."

Jessica and Blackie followed close behind him. Before them another puff of smoke rose from the hills.

The three scouts watching the three travelers argued about what to do.

"You must ride to the stronghold and tell Maco." The leader pointed to the two braves. "I will stay and watch the White-Eyes."

"We could kill them now," the younger warrior said.

"No, we are not a raiding party—just lookouts." He shook his lance at the brave. "Do what I say."

"You are right," the older warrior said. "Maco and White Horse are the avengers. They will take care of the white men."

"Go then."

The two Apaches rode off toward their encampment.

Jake led Blackie and Jessica to the south of the smoke signal. Once inside a small patch of cottonwoods, they stopped.

"These trees will cover us for a time." Jake dis-mounted. "Let the horses rest.

May need all their strength before long."

Jessica held her pinto's reins. "Will they attack us?"

"Hard to say." Jake went to the edge of the trees. "Don't know how many of them there are."

Blackie tied Ace to a branch, took his rifle, and stood next to Jake. "If there was more than two or three, I'd think they'd be beatin' down on us by now."

"You may be right," Jake said. "If their camp is close, you can bet more will be coming."

"Then, I say we make a break for it." Blackie started back to his horse.

"Hold on." Jake raised his hand. "If it's the same bunch who raided the town, we might stand a chance by telling them the man who killed the Apache boy is dead and his store burned to the ground."

Blackie turned. "I don't think they'd believe you."

"Their chief could have killed me, but he didn't."

"He may get another chance. Look." Blackie pointed.

A large cloud of dust was closing on them.

"Come on!" Jake waved and jumped on his stallion.

Jessica followed, then Blackie bounded on Ace. They lit out the other side of the cottonwoods before the Apaches got to the trees.

Maco and White Horse, armed with shields and rifles, led the eight Apache warriors into the trees.

"They must not escape." Maco thrust his shield into the air.

White Horse, riding beside him, spurred his horse on. "My boy's spirit must have peace."

They gained on the woman and two men. Maco sent four warriors around the outskirts of the cottonwood grove to cut off their escape.

Jake urged Sam to a full gallop and turned north into the hills. Jessica and Blackie followed just as the four braves rounded a bend in the trail. They shot arrows that missed their marks.

"Head for those rocks up ahead!" Jake swatted his horse with the reins.

The three of them charged behind an outcrop of jagged stones and jumped off their horses.

Jake pulled his rifle from its sheath. "I'll take the first one. You take the second." He motioned to Blackie.

Jessica ducked behind a big rock. "I can shoot. Throw me a gun."

"Here." Jake tossed her his .44, then shot off a round at one of the charging Apaches.

The Indian sank to the ground, wounded. The other warriors spread out and attacked from three sides. Blackie took aim and was about to pull his rifle's trigger when an arrow pierced his right shoulder. Jake whirled around, shot the Apache in the chest.

Jessica bolted to Blackie and shielded him with her body. "Lie still."

The other two Apaches reined in their horses behind rocks across from Jake.

"Stay down." Jake motioned to Jessica. "I'll take their fire." He raised his rifle, leveled it toward the hostiles.

"Blackie's bleeding pretty bad." Jessica took hold of the arrow in his shoulder.

Jake waved. "Leave it in."

"I thought I should try and pull it out. It might be poisoned. He's not conscious."

"He may bleed to death if you pull it out." He fired his rifle at the concealed Apaches.

As he turned back to her, Maco, White Horse, and the other two Apaches leaped into their hiding place with rifles trained on Jake, Jessica, and the wounded Blackie.

CHAPTER FIFTEEN

Maco, wild-eyed, stood tall and waved his rifle at Jake, who eased his finger off the trigger of his rifle and slowly put it on the ground. Jessica jerked up from Blackie, saw it was Maco standing over them, and reached for Blackie's gun. Maco stuck his rifle in her neck. She stopped. Jake rose, but two warriors restrained him.

In Apache, Maco told his raiders to bind them. He took their weapons and kicked Blackie in the ribs to stir him. Blackie groaned, opened his eyes. Through the blurriness, he saw the situation and tried to rise. The marauders tied his hands, dragged him to his feet with the arrow still in him.

"Looks like we're going to their camp," Jake said.

Jessica twisted away from a brave's grip. "Do you think he recognizes us?"

"Yeah, he does." Jake looked at Maco waving for the other four Apaches to come across the opening. "He could've killed me during the raid on the town, but didn't."

"I don't think he'll be that kind now." She was pushed toward a horse and lifted onto its back.

Maco cracked a thin smile as he watched her struggle. *He did remember this pretty white woman who slept close to him once. What would happen when it happened again? She must not escape again.*

Jake, hands tied in the front, swung up on his horse. The Apaches put Blackie across his saddle, climbed aboard their ponies, and headed out of the pocket of rocks.

Maco led the riders at a slow pace until they reached the outer boundaries of their stronghold. The lookouts waved to him. Maco raised his rifle and pumped it twice in the air. He let out a victory cry and led his captors into the encampment.

Blackie was taken down from his horse by two braves and put into a wickiup. Maco sent two women and the Medicine

Man to treat him. The Medicine Man pulled the arrow out of his right shoulder and applied a paste of mixed herbs to the wound after the women washed it.

Jake was tied to a tree not far from the central fire pit. Three women, following Maco's command, pulled Jessica off her horse and thrust her into his wickiup

Susan Blackhawk, walking back to camp from a close-by pond, saw the white woman. "Who is that?" She approached Maco.

"She is a hostage like the two white men." He turned to her.

"Must she be put in our wickiup?"

"It is my wickiup." His tone left no room for argument.

"Yes, it is. I just thought . . ."

His eyes bore into her. "I will sell her for many rifles."

"That is good, but do not keep her."

"Do you dare make decisions for me?"

Susan backed away. "No—no—you are the leader.   I . . ."

"Enough! Finish your chores."

Susan turned and disappeared around a wickiup.

Jake watched the two of them from his confinement. He could not understand what they said, but saw the expressions on their faces. *She didn't look Apache. A pretty woman. Was she the chief's woman? Or was she a captive also? She didn't look too happy when she left.*

He continued to survey the scene.

Maco looked at him once, then walked away.

Jake struggled with his bonds behind his back, but the restraints were tied securely. He pulled against the tree scraping the insides of his arms through his shirt. Relaxing, he scanned the camp to get a better bearing where he was. Just as he figured out the best escape route, several women and children gathered around him and started throwing small stones at him. He ducked his head to protect his eyes, but did not cry out when the rocks hit him. The women laughed and the children whooped war chants as they threw more stones at him. Loose dogs barked and snapped at him.

Maco, hearing the commotion, stuck his head out of his wickiup and realized what was going on. He bolted out, rushed to Jake's attackers, and raised his hand. The women stopped taunting at Jake and held the children back.

"This man is my prisoner, my hostage," he spoke in Apache. "He is not to be treated like a common Mexican scalp hunter."

The women and children dropped their missiles and backed away. Maco surveyed the welts on Jake's face and head. Just as he turned to fetch a woman, he saw Susan Blackhawk walking back into camp.

"Come." He waved to her. "Get some water. Cleanse this white man's bumps."

She looked at him and at Jake for a moment. *Each man had features she liked, but the one tied up was a white man—the enemy.* She hesitated, but Maco motioned again. This time she picked up a water bag near the fire and walked toward Jake.

Jake watched her approach. *She was a beautiful young Indian woman. Her eyes were dark, but not black like the Apaches. She was taller than most Apaches. Her skin was smooth and lighter in color than the Apaches. She must be Cheyenne with maybe some white thrown in.* Jake stared the closer she came.

Susan stopped in front of him and examined the abrasions. She held the water bag in her left hand and dipped a piece of cloth into it, then gently pressed the wet cloth on Jake's forehead.

The cool compress shook him out of his trance; he stared into her eyes. She repeated the soothing dressing several times all the while concentrating on the handsome enemy. *He was tall, rugged, had strong features almost like a Cheyenne warrior. She felt a certain magnetism, like the first time she saw Maco.* Then she snapped back and was done, but stood in front of Jake for a moment before she walked away.

Jake gazed after her until she disappeared into Maco's wickiup. He twisted his bound wrists, but the ropes held tight. After a few minutes, he relaxed. *He'd bide his time—wait until the opportunity came to escape. What about Jessica and Blackie?*

Jessica, sitting on a fur, looked up when Susan Blackhawk entered Maco's wickiup. She hadn't noticed the young maiden before and marveled at how pretty she was compared to the other Apache women. Susan gave her a quick stinging glance and moved to the rear of the wickiup.

Maco returned a short time later and felt the hostility between the two women. *Here he was, leader of the band. Two handsome women in his grasp. He could take either one at any time, but something inside told him that wouldn't do. They would have to want him. It was easier to kill enemies.*

He looked at Susan Blackhawk. She did not return his glare. He looked at Jessica. She sought his eyes. "What do you want with me?"

Maco did not understand what she said, but Susan knew a little English and let a sardonic smile cross her lips. He saw her face and scowled. *Was she making fun of a great warrior?*

She drew back and Maco turned to Jessica. "You are my prize to sell or keep," he said in Apache.

Jessica saw the tenacity in his eyes and understood what he meant. *He had her captive once before. She would have to wait and see.*

That night, after the Apache women crushed corn, soaked it, and allowed it to ferment into an intoxicating juice called tis-win, the warriors drank and danced celebrating their captive hostages. The campfire grew higher the longer they drank and danced.

One younger brave drank too much, got disoriented, and wandered off. He sat against a pine tree in a stupor trying to get his bearings when a hungry mountain lion pounced on him from a rocky ledge. The brave screamed, rolled over, and pulled a knife from his waist. He lashed out at the lion, but the animal was too quick and avoided the thrusts. Teeth flashing, the cat charged slashing its large paws at the Apache. The brave, alert now, fought back with his knife and cut the lion several times before the lion caught him and tore at his scalp. Blood poured off his head, but he kept sticking the knife into the cat. Growling and backing up, the lion struck out with his claws until a fallen tree trunk stopped it. The warrior thrust his knife into the mountain lion's hide so many times the cat turned, leaped over the tree, and ran away. The exhausted brave slumped down on his knees, caught his breath, and wiped at his bloody face. He stuck a hand into the top of his head and pulled out sticky fingers. He licked his hand, but suddenly felt dizzy and faint. Shaking his head, he crawled toward the camp.

When Maco saw the bloody warrior reach the camp's edge, he raised his right hand. The dancing stopped. Some of the drunken Apaches wavered and fell. Several women rushed over and cradled the wounded man in their arms. Maco stood over them and motioned to the Medicine Man.

Jake watched as the young brave related his ordeal to Maco and the band. Then they carried him to a wickiup so the Medicine Man could administer his herbs and treatment.

Some of the elders and a few young braves approached Maco.

"It is a bad omen," the oldest elder said. "The white people have provoked the spirits."

White Horse joined them. "It is true, my brother. We should have burned the whole town and killed all the White-Eyes."

Maco saw the fire in his eyes. "Porico, this white man could have killed me, but didn't." He pointed to Jake.

"He may still do it unless we take his scalp now."

"No. I am leader. I will decide what to do." Maco raised his right hand. "Now, go. It is late. All of you go."

Slowly, they backed off and went to their wickiups. Maco glanced at Jake, then walked away.

Jake watched him disappear. *Now, what was that all about? They didn't look too happy. A disagreement of some sort. Maybe about our fate. He had to escape somehow, and soon.*

Later that night, White Horse crept out of his wickiup, gripped his hunting knife tightly and headed for Jake. *The white man must die.*

CHAPTER SIXTEEN

Jake, weary eyed, head slumped down, heard a twig snap. He jerked up, focused on the sound. White Horse crouched behind a rock on the far side of the campfire. He scanned the whole area for any movement, then approached Jake from the rear. Jake, alert now, heard the stirring and twisted his head to the side. He saw nothing, but he stiffened. He felt another's presence. White Horse rushed from his hiding place toward Jake. He raised the knife; ready to plunge it into Jake when a strong hand grabbed his arm and shook the knife loose.

"You are not to kill the white man, Porico." Maco held his grip tight. "He is mine to kill if I choose."

"But, the omen, brother. It is bad." White Horse let his arm go limp. "First, my son is killed, now another Apache is attacked by a mountain lion."

"I do not believe a evil spirit did those things." Maco released his grip.

White Horse stood straight. "Is the great Maco growing weak? Maybe a new leader is needed."

"My brother, you should know I am not weak, but if you seek a new leader, will you go against me?"

White Horse saw the fierceness on Maco's face. He stepped back a few paces. "I will not oppose you."

"Good, then we will go back to our wickiups now and sleep the rest of the night." He picked up White Horse's knife and handed it to him.

White Horse took it and slowly walked away. Maco turned to Jake and examined his bonds. He pulled on the rawhide to make sure they were tight.

Jake met his eyes. "Gracias—thank you."

Maco knew some Spanish and nodded. Then he walked away.

Jake took a deep breath. *Whew, that was close. What's with this Apache leader? He could kill us any time. They are raiders—killers. The more they kill, the greater their prestige. He must want us for bigger game.* He stared into the campfire until his eyes grew heavy and he drifted into a restless sleep.

The next morning, Blackie stirred from deep slumber brought on by the Medicine Man's herbs to combat the pain of the wound. His blurry eyes focused after a few blinks and he saw he was alone in a wickiup. External herbs were wrapped underneath rawhide on his injured shoulder. He moved his arm slightly and felt no pain. *Jake—Jessica—where are they? Last thing he remembered—Jessica holding him, looking at the arrow sticking out of his shoulder.* He put his right hand down his right side, but felt no gun. His shirt was torn at the sleeve and he looked around for something to use as a sling. The wickiup was dark, but a touch of light entered through a slit in the front flap. Blackie sat up, crawled to the opening, and peered out. Dawn's early gray streaks gave him enough light to see Jake tied to a tree on the other side of the campfire. *Damn! Didn't he cut Jake free once before. The man must love trouble.* He moved backward, scanned the wickiup for his gun and a knife. Many scalps hung from poles and animal furs adorned the area. He searched underneath fur robes and blankets until he found a hunting knife. Across the room he saw the buckle of his gunbelt and strapped it on. Blackie opened the flap a crack, surveyed the campsite, and saw no one was up yet. He quietly stole around to the left of the wickiups until he was in the trees behind Jake. Blackie pulled the knife and approached the tied-up man.

Jake heard the movement behind him. "Who . . .?" He turned his head.

"Quiet, it's me, Blackie," he whispered.

"How did you get free?"

"Just woke up. Nobody was around. I'm gonna cut you loose." He sliced the rawhide and freed Jake's hands, then handed the knife to Jake. "Here, you get your feet."

Jake rubbed his wrists for a moment, then cut the bonds around his feet. "Do you know where Jessica is?"

"No, but we'll have to leave her."

"We can't leave her."

"We have to. They won't kill her. She's too valuable."

"But, he'll take her." Jake frowned.

"He—you mean the chief."

"Yeah, the big one."

"Well, she's been taken before, if that's what's bothering you."

"I don't . . ."

Blackie stood firm. "Look, we get out of here now or they kill us."

"We gotta find her."

"We'll come back for her. Get some help and come back."

Jake moved closer to the trees. "All right, find a couple of horses."

"They're tethered over this way." Blackie led the way.

When they got to the horses, all was quiet. There were no guards. They picked out their horses, strapped on the saddles, and rode out of the stronghold.

The lookouts on top of the rocks near the canyon's mouth saw the two riders pass. One of the warriors ran back to camp and awakened Maco. "The white men have escaped."

"How did that happen?" He rushed over to the tree where Jake had been tied and saw the cut rawhide laying on the ground. "The wounded one must have done this."

"Do we go after them?" the brave asked.

"No. We have their woman. They will be back."

Jessica woke up amid the commotion of the other tribesmen gathering around Maco. She crawled to the opening and peered out. Maco stood in the middle of everyone, speaking and gesturing. She watched them until they broke up and Maco headed back to his wickiup. She hurried back to her furs.

Susan Blackhawk was gone doing her morning chores when Maco entered the wickiup. Jessica pretended to be asleep. He pulled down the buffalo robe covering her and exposed her naked body. She lay there with her arms across her chest trying not to shiver from the cold. He stared at her lithe lines for several moments until she opened her eyes and pulled the robe back up.

"What are you doing?" She glared at him, eyes flashing.

He seemed to understand and backed away. In Spanish, he said, "Your men have escaped."

Jessica understood him and sighed. *They left her—on her own—surely they would come back for her.* She sat up, her face twisted, her eyes blank.

Maco strode out of the wickiup and headed for the campfire. Susan Blackhawk scooped up a plate of beans and presented it to him. He took it, peered into her eyes. *Two such beauties— how could he choose? Why choose? Why not take both of them?* A warm stirring pierced his insides. He turned away, sat down, and ate his food.

Susan watched him while he ate. *She had been with him for a while now. He had not taken her, but the feelings were there. This she knew. She imagined what he would do. He would be rugged, detached, take his fill of her without a word. She was his prize, to do what he would. She felt the hot blood rushing through her, but could not be the one to approach first. Apaches did not put their mouths together as she had seen her father do to her mother. Now, there's the other woman—the white one. He sometimes looked at her the way he had when they first met. The white woman must die.*

CHAPTER SEVENTEEN

Jake and Blackie reined up their horses at a small stream several miles from the Apache stronghold.

"Looks like they're not coming after us." Jake dismounted.

"Mighty strange. I was sure they'd be on us." Blackie let Ace drink the cool water.

Jake led Sam to the water. "That Apache leader isn't dumb. He knows we'll come back for Jessica."

"How we gonna do it? The town was almost wiped out. Where will we find some men?"

"I don't know yet. We may have to find a fort?"

"You mean the cavalry?"

Jake stuck a hand in the stream, splashed water on his face. "Maybe, but then again, if we get rearmed, two men might stand a better chance."

"You're crazy." Blackie shook his head. "We were lucky back there—and my shoulder's still bad."

"Then I'll go alone."

Blackie stared at Jake. "You want Jessica that much?"

"I'd do the same for you."

"Yeah, I guess you would." Blackie remounted. "We better get going."

Jake patted Sam's neck. "You're right. That shoulder of yours needs some attention."

"And we need some guns, partner."

Jake smiled as they rode toward Adobe Crossing.

When they arrived in town they saw the burned-out ruins from the Apache attack. Jake reined up in front of the sheriff's office, which was spared. He dismounted, walked inside, and found the rifle rack. Blackie followed him in.

"I'm taking a couple rifles and a six-gun," Jake said. "Gonna head out in the morning."

Blackie examined another rifle and searched the desk drawers for pistols. "We'll need some shells."

"So, you're going along for sure?"

"Yeah, the doc can bandage up my shoulder good enough. Seems those Apache herbs work pretty well."

Jake turned. "The shells are on that wall over there."

* * * *

Maco held council with the elders and the young warriors after he finished eating. Many braves were angry over the two white men's escape. They wanted another raid on the town. The elders sat and smoked.

"Patience, my young ones." Maco rose. "We will have our day. Those men will return and may bring others with them. We will be waiting."

White Horse raised a hand. "Hear my brother. We have a prize hostage and she will command big medicine. The White-Eyes will fall into our trap."

"Porico and I have spoken," Maco said. "We will prepare to take the white men's scalps."

The warriors yipped, chanted, and started dancing. Maco watched for a few minutes, then retreated to his wickiup. Jessica was up and dressed when he entered. He spread his right hand forward and across his body as if to say 'sit'.

She understood and crouched down. *Thank God she wasn't tied up any longer. Now, what was she going to do with her? He had seen her naked, but didn't do anything to her. Was he trying to gain her trust or just waiting for the right weak moment? What would she do? She had known only one lover. He was handsome in a savage way.*

Maco stood before her. In Apache, he spoke to her. "Your men left you. They are cowards. If they come back, they will be tortured very slowly and scalped."

Jessica held out her hands and shrugged. She did not understand him, but saw from the look in his deep black eyes that he could kill.

Maco motioned her to stand, then he went to his war paint, dipped two fingers in it, and spread a wide white strip across

82

his nose and cheeks. Jessica stepped back as he grabbed a rifle and a lance and strode out the entrance flap.

* * * *

After resting their horses for two days, Jake and Blackie saddled up in the early morning and headed out of Adobe Crossing toward the Apache stronghold.

"I still think we should have brought some men with us," Blackie said.

Jake looked at him. "The Apaches will be watching for a group of men. The two of us have a better chance of getting through their lines."

"I hope so. If we don't get Jessica out, she'll be taken as the chief's wife."

"She may have been already."

"You're right. She may have been." Blackie spurred his horse.

Jake caught up with him. "Racing the horses won't do any good. We'll need their reserve strength on the way back."

"Have you figured out how we're gonna do it?"

"First thing—we've got to get past the lookouts."

"We'll do that at night. It's our best chance."

They pressed on toward the mountains not saying much more. As they left the desert floor, the sky darkened. The wind picked up and large raindrops pelted the riders.

"Perfect," Jake said. "This downpour will provide our cover."

Thunder boomed and lightning cracked through the sky. Their horses shied, but Jake and Blackie tightened the reins and controlled their stallions.

"We better head for a rocky overhang and hole up a while." Blackie kicked Ace's sides and the horse bolted forward.

Jake followed him to a canyon entrance. "Over there." He pointed.

They reined up as lightning hit around them.

"Watch that wash," Jake said. "If it keeps raining hard that'll be a wild torrent."

"We'll have to go around the rocks, up another way." Blackie leaned on his saddle horn.

"The lookouts won't expect that and we can take them out."

"A knife won't make much noise."

"Specially in a storm." Jake adjusted his wet hat.

* * * *

The rain came down hard as Maco prepared his warriors for their ambush. "We will wait now. The White-Eyes won't come in this storm. Go back to your wickiups and wait. The guards will warn us if danger comes."

They dispersed in different directions. Maco took his lance and rifle back to his wickiup.

Jessica was alone when he entered. Susan Blackhawk was with some of the older women in a large wickiup nearby.

Jessica looked up from the fire pit. Maco glistened in the light; his bare muscular chest caught her attention and she fixated on him. He stared back, watched her eyes survey his body and moved closer to her. She did not back up. He took her hand, drew her to him. She felt his wetness and shivered. It was not a shiver of cold, but of excitement. Maco pressed closer to her. She felt his manhood hard between her legs and dug her fingers into his back. Rising on her toes, she tilted her lips to his, but he did not know what to do. Then she opened her mouth and pressed against his. He tasted her warm lips, a sensation he had not known before. His hands glided from her waist to her breasts and he squeezed harder than she had experienced. She let out a gasp and he eased back, but still held her bosom. Jessica tugged at his breechcloth and slid it down past his knees. He tore at her clothes until she stood naked in his arms. Lowering to a buffalo robe, he entered her. She tried to slow his thrusts, but could not, so she met every penetration with her own movement until they released their juices.

Maco rolled off her and stared at the ceiling of the wickiup. Rain beat down on the roof. Jessica gazed into the fire.

After a few minutes of rest Maco reached for her again. She turned to him just as the entrance flap opened and Susan Blackhawk entered.

CHAPTER EIGHTEEN

Jessica pulled the robe up to her neck. Maco lay wide-eyed staring at Susan Blackhawk.

She stalked over to them. "White bitch, what have you done? He is mine!"

Her native Cheyenne tongue stung Jessica's ears even though she could not understand her.

Maco slipped on his breechcloth and stood. "Woman—a great warrior needs more than one."

"I was to be more to you than anyone." Susan picked up a pot and threw it at him.

He caught it before it hit his head and set it on the ground. Jessica moved back against a wall and struggled under the robe to put on her clothes.

"You will be my first wife," Maco edged toward Susan. "When I found you, I knew it the first moment."

"Then why did you take this White-Eyes?" She pointed to Jessica.

"It is a warrior's right. It has nothing to do with you."

Susan threw her arms into the air. "I thought the Apache was more honorable." She turned and burst outside.

Jessica sat with her mouth open. Maco stared at the entrance for a few moments, then turned to Jessica.

"My actions cannot be questioned. I am war chief." He walked outside also.

Jessica gazed after him. *What did she do? She wanted him. He wanted her.*

That pretty maiden thought she was his alone. Could there ever be just one for each of them? Jessica shuddered. *The Cheyenne would surely kill her.*

* * * *

The storm still raged when Jake and Blackie saddled up to attack the Apache stronghold. Torrents of water gushed down the canyon's entrance so the two men urged their stallions around and through the side rocks. Near the top they stopped and peered into the deluge looking for the Apache lookouts.

"They're probably sheltered somewhere under a ledge," Jake said.

"If we can't see them, they won't be able to see or hear us." Blackie patted Ace's neck.

Jake turned. "Don't be too sure. The Apache are masters of hidden tactics."

"Better get on with it then." Blackie nudged Ace with his boot.

Jake followed. "Right."

They started down the other side when Jake suddenly stopped. He motioned to Blackie. "Down there." He pointed to a small fire on the side of the hill.

"I see him."

"Only one. The other one must be on the far side of the draw." Jake dismounted, tied Sam to a tree branch. "Blackie, you stay here."

Jake took out his knife and made his way down between the rocks. The lookout was under a ledge resting against a boulder with his feet near the campfire. Jake crept toward him staying in the shadows. The drenching rain beat on the rocks around the warrior's post. Jake picked up a rock and threw it to the other side of the Apache. The brave jerked up with the sound of the rock striking against another rock. He looked all around the area, but saw nothing except the storm. Lightning fractured a nearby tree and in the burst of light, the lookout saw Jake's outline. But, it was too late. Jake swept down on him, slashed his knife into the Apache's chest. The man fell backward, Jake on top of him. Blood poured from the wound as the brave's eyes rolled. Jake pushed back, regained his feet, and pulled out his knife. He stepped close to the fire, waved for Blackie to come down.

"The next one's mine." Blackie leaped from his mount.

"I don't think we'll have to worry about the other one. He's across the canyon. The water's too strong to ford."

"Then we better get into their camp."

"Everyone should be in the wickiups during this storm."

"That's right, but which one holds Jessica?"

"The one with the chief."

Blackie looked at him. "That may be a problem."

"We knew that all along."

"Doesn't make it any easier."

Jake pondered a moment. "A diversion. You go after the horses. Cut them loose. That should start a big mess."

"Then you'll go against him by yourself?"

"Yeah, but I've got surprise on my side."

Blackie scratched his forehead. "You may need more than that."

"Thanks for the encouragement." Jake smiled. "Let's get it done."

The two men rode farther into the canyon until they spotted the group of wickiups. The Apache horses were tethered to the right of the camp in a grove of trees. Rain pelted the area relentlessly and Jake motioned to Blackie to head for the horses. Then Jake walked Ace behind an outlying wickiup and swung down from his saddle. The only sound he heard was rain beating the roofs and the ground. He smelled smoke coming from the wickiups and crept between the huts.

Blackie reined up near the horses, dismounted, and tied Ace to a tree. He started to cut the Apache horses free when he saw a lone figure sitting on a stump facing the opposite direction. Blackie pulled his knife, approached the Indian with it poised to strike. Just as he raised the knife for the kill, the Indian turned to him. Blackie almost dropped the weapon. Before him as lightning belched, sat a beautiful young woman, soaking wet. She shivered from the cold and rain, but did not move. He sheathed his knife, but grabbed her by the dress. Now she struggled, flailing at his chest with her fists. He took her lashes, twisted her arms, and subdued her. She kicked at him and started to yell when he gagged her mouth with his hand. "I hate to do this, but you leave me no choice." He pulled his pistol and conked her on the head just enough to put her down without drawing blood. Susan Blackhawk sank to the muddy ground. Blackie tied her hands with a bandanna, then cut the horses free. They ran in all directions, galloped through and around the camp. The Apache men, hearing the stampede, bolted out of their wickiups. Most of the horses were too fast or slippery to catch and the warriors huddled around Maco who looked on in disbelief.

"The White-Eyes!" Maco raised his fist. "Get your lances, your rifles."

Jake hid behind a wickiup. He watched which hut Maco entered, then slid in back of it. Maco rushed out again in a few seconds with a rifle, gave a war cry, and sent his men in all directions.

Jake inched around to the entrance, slipped under the flap. Jessica sat beside the fire, staring at the entrance.

"Jessica," he whispered. "Come on. Let's go."

She blinked, startled. "Jake! Where did you—How?"

"Never mind. You're free. Give me your hand."

"But—what about Blackie?"

"He's waiting." Jake pulled her to him, shoved her out the entrance into the rain.

The Apaches ran around the entire camp trying to catch their horses. Jake and Jessica headed for the trees where the horses were tethered.

Blackie swung Susan Blackhawk onto a horse when he saw Jake and Jessica. They lunged for their horses and the four of them galloped toward the canyon's flooded entrance.

Blackie held the reins to Susan's horse as they raced along the swollen water. No shouts or cries followed them. He eased up near the canyon's mouth until a bullet whizzed past his head. *The other lookout. He forgot about him.* Blackie pointed up to Jake and zigzagged the two horses.

Jake unloaded a few rounds from his pistol toward the lookout to keep his attention. Jessica ducked low in her saddle and followed him, but her horse slipped in the mud and plunged into the roaring water. She flew from the saddle into the surging torrent and disappeared under the waves.

Jake pulled Sam up, sliding several feet. By the time he turned, Jessica rushed past him, her head bobbing up and down. He spurred Sam and galloped downstream after Jessica and her horse.

Blackie had stopped ahead of them, grabbed a lariat from his saddle horn, and threw it at Jessica. She reached for it, but could not catch it. Jake thundered by, drove Sam into the water, and jumped off toward Jessica. He lashed out, caught her leg, and jerked her his way. Pulling hard, he managed to drag her toward the water's edge.

Exhausted and gasping for breath, she turned on her back and rested in Jake's arms. Both soaked to the skin, they gazed at each other for a few moments, breathing heavily. He clutched her like a doll and bent his lips to her. She took his mouth in hers and they embraced in the pelting rain.

CHAPTER NINETEEN

Jessica broke away. "Jake—thanks."

"You don't have to thank me."

"Yes, I do, but I should tell you . . ."

He rose to his knees. "Tell me later. We've got to catch your horse."

"All right, but it's important."

Jake stood, helped her up.

"I caught him." Blackie rode back with her horse. "He's pretty tired."

"We'd better rest a spell." Jake pointed to a rocky ledge.

Blackie turned. "Good idea. I'll get my captive."

"Captive?"

"You won't believe it." He trotted down to where he tied Susan Blackhawk to a tree.

Jake and Jessica and their horses stood in the rock shelter when Blackie rode back with Susan. She started to gain consciousness, but was blurry-eyed and sore from the knock on the head.

"She's a beauty." Blackie lifted her head, showed them her face.

"Certainly is," Jake said, "but why do you have her?"

"She was by the horses. Had to take her or kill her. Couldn't kill her."

Jake scratched his head. "Might be a good trade sometime."

"That's what I thought." Blackie helped her down from her horse.

Jessica went to her. "She's not a thing. She's the leader's woman, a maiden."

"Cheyenne." Susan placed her hand against her chest. "Maco's woman until the white one came."

"She's Cheyenne?" Jake asked. "What's she doing with the Apache?"

Blackie looked up at the dwindling rain. "We'll have to get her story later. We better get out of here now. Those Apaches will be after us when they find out who's missing."

"You're right. Get mounted." Jake swung up on Sam.

Jessica followed. Blackie set Susan on her horse and mounted Ace. They rode out of the canyon as the water subsided.

* * * *

Maco and the other warriors captured most of the horses as the storm passed. He posted more guards around the stronghold with orders to shoot any intruders. Then he went back to his wickiup. When he walked in he saw the hut was empty; he turned around and rushed outside. He called for the older women of the band to hunt for Jessica and Susan Blackhawk. After many minutes, they reported no one had seen the two young women.

Maco stalked back into his wickiup. "The tall white man! I should have killed him. His scalp would be on my lodge pole now."

White Horse entered. "They are gone?"

"See for yourself."

White Horse saw the fire in Maco's eyes. "We must raid again. This time, no mercy. We will burn the rest of the town, scalp all the whites."

"Good. I want those two women back. I will hunt down the tall man." Maco tied his war band around his head.

* * * *

Slight-pink streaks of dawn opened the sky as Jake, Jessica, Blackie, and Susan Blackhawk walked their horses down Adobe Crossing's main street. They reined up in front of the sheriff's office and dismounted. Blackie helped Susan off her horse. She rubbed her still-tied hands and shook grogginess from her head.

"We better dig up some grub," Jake said.

"Where?" Blackie asked.

Jessica looked up and down the street. "The boarding house. It's still standing.

"All right. Let's go." Jake led the way.

Blackie took Susan by the arm.

"Does she still have to be tied up?" Jessica walked beside them. "She was one of the leader's women."

Blackie's eyes widened. "One of his women? How many does he have?"

"I don't know." Jessica turned away.

Jake glanced back at them. Jessica did not meet his eyes. Susan Blackhawk shifted her eyes to Jessica. Jake caught the drift and continued walking.

Lamplight shone through the windows as they approached the boarding house.

"Looks like they're awake in there," Jake said.

Blackie rubbed his stomach. "Now if they set a big table."

"Are you going to untie her?" Jessica touched his arm.

"I guess so." He turned, unbound his captive. "Now you behave."

Susan nodded. "I'm hungry." She patted her stomach.

"She understood," Blackie said.

After a flapjack breakfast, Jake and Blackie paid the lady of the house and they and the two women walked back to the sheriff's office.

Susan Blackhawk felt better after food. Her head still ached, but she did not give in to the pain. *She was Cheyenne. Apaches and whites would never conquer her, though she found Maco, Jake, and Blackie easy to look at. This tall man in black found her sitting on a stump in the rain. Maco had cast her aside in favor of the white woman. Cheyennes did not feel sorry for themselves. They vented revenge on enemies, but the woman inside her seethed with passion for the Apache leader. She would wait until it was time to escape and return to him. He would want her again—this she knew.* She followed Blackie into the office.

Jessica halted Jake outside.

"Something on your mind?" he asked.

She looked into his blue eyes. "That kiss, back in the canyon—did it just happen or had you thought about it a while?"

"I thought about it since you rode behind me to Adobe Crossing after the stage was attacked."

"I thought so. Guess I imagined it also, but . . ."

"But you don't want to carry it any further?"

"Not exactly. I just need to tell you something." She cast her eyes downward.

"Can't be that bad."

"It's the reason Blackie has the Cheyenne . . ." She hesitated. "The night you and Blackie escaped, Maco came to me. I didn't have much choice. Remember I told you about the one lover I had—the sea captain. That was long ago, then I met Blackie and you. I don't know what I'm trying to say, but I had to tell you."

Jake stepped back. "That one kiss triggered all this. Mighty powerful."

"I know. Hope you can forgive me."

"Nothing to forgive. You're a woman—have the same needs as any man."

"I was hoping you'd understand."

"I understand our bodies need fulfillment—man or woman. After Ella left me, I still needed the physical contact with a woman."

Jessica moved close to him and put her hands around his neck. She tilted her mouth to his and pulled him to her in a long embrace.

That evening after dinner, the two men and two women found lodging in the boarding house. Sleep came fast for all of them in separate rooms.

Jake woke before dawn. He heard hooves pounding up and down Main Street. When he looked out the window, a flaming arrow flew into the side of the house.

CHAPTER TWENTY

Jake threw on his shirt, pants, and gunbelt. He ran down the hall, banged on the doors. "The Apaches! House is on fire! Get up!"

Blackie flew out of his room, slammed open Susan Blackhawk's door. She was still tied to the bed. "Come on—the Apaches are attacking." He untied her.

She leaped out of bed and followed him. "Maco—he's come for me."

Blackie grabbed her hand, pulled her to him. "You stay with me."

She looked up at the big man. "Until it is time."

"Time?" He did not get an answer. Flames shot out of a front bedroom. "Downstairs, quick."

Jake and Jessica were already at the front door when Blackie and Susan arrived.

He halted them and others coming down the stairs. "Better go out the back way."

Outside, everyone dispersed. Jake led his three companions behind buildings toward the sheriff's office. "We need more firepower."

"I'll take a shotgun," Blackie said.

On the front side of the buildings, the Apaches torched whatever they hit and killed whoever ran out. They whooped, yelped, and charged up and down the street spewing fire and death.

Jake was the first one in the sheriff's office and snatched a rifle from the wall case. Blackie grabbed a shotgun. Both men took positions at the front window. The women crouched behind the desk.

"Stay down." Jake motioned.

"I need a pistol," Jessica said.

"There's one in the desk drawer."

Blackie looked at him. "What about the girl?"

"You take care of her."

Blackie reached for his pistol, but stopped before he took it out of the holster. "Best you just stick close to me." He waved her to him.

"I will not kill my comrades." Susan Blackhawk crawled from behind the desk to Blackie's side.

"I hope they feel the same way about you." Blackie ducked as an arrow shattered the window, just missing her.

Jake lowered his head. "Everybody stay down. They may start shooting flaming arrows at us."

"Maybe we should get out the back way," Jessica said.

"Too dangerous. Too many of them." Jake leveled his rifle at a horseman in the street.

"What if they rush us?"

"Then we'll make a break out the back."

Susan had been kneeling next to Blackie for several minutes peering through the broken front window. Without warning, she lunged for the door and bolted outside. Blackie dropped his rifle, dove after her. She landed on the front steps with him right behind her. An Apache raider, riding hard, aimed his bow as she turned. Blackie jumped in front of her at the same time the arrow left the bow. He pushed her aside, took the

arrow in his left shoulder, and fell to the ground. Susan stayed down until the warrior rode past, then turned to Blackie. She started to pull the arrow out.

"Wait," he said.

"You saved me. I must help you."

"You were going back to them."

"Yes, but they tried to kill me."

Blackie moaned. "I know the feeling."

"I want my own people, the Cheyenne."

"Then help me back inside."

She dragged him toward the steps. Jake opened the office door and helped her get Blackie inside just as arrows hit the door.

With Blackie lying on his back, Jake broke the arrow shaft and pulled it out of his shoulder. Blood poured out of the wound, but Susan found a towel on a hook and held it down on his shoulder.

Everyone was paying attention to Blackie when the back door opened and Maco burst in. He trained a rifle on them and grunted.

Jake looked up. "What the . . .?"

Maco waved the rifle, motioning for Jessica to come to him. She watched his blazing eyes for a few moments, then moved toward him. Jake went for his pistol, but Maco shot it out of his right hand.

"Someday, I will take your scalp," Maco said, "but now I take your woman." He grabbed Jessica and dragged her out the back door.

Susan Blackhawk looked on with her mouth open. *He does not want me. It is time*

for me to go back to my people. She pressed the towel harder on Blackie and gazed into his glazed eyes. "You are a brave man, white man, You saved my life. I will not forget."

He groaned, stared back at this beautiful Indian maiden who kept him from bleeding to death. A whisper emitted from his lips. "Thank you . . ."

Jake grabbed a rifle, rushed out the back door. Maco and Jessica were gone.

Maco urged his pony to a full gallop. Jessica clung to his bare back, her hands and arms wrapped tightly around his chest. He felt her breasts soft against him as they rode toward his stronghold.

She pressed her head against his neck. *What would he do with her? Was he going to kill her now that he had her again? Or would he bed her again? He was crude that first time, but she felt a passion she had not known before. And Jake—he was sure to come after them. Then what? A fight to the death—for her?*

Jake peered out the sheriff's office door. Several buildings roared in flames. A few bodies lay along the wooden walkway and in the street. *Not as bad as he thought. A diversion—to take back Jessica. They could have taken the whole town to its knees.* He stepped back.

Blackie's head lay in Susan Blackhawk's lap now. His eyes were focused and he moved his legs.

"We better get you to a room and a doctor," Jake said.

Blackie lifted his head. "Feels pretty good right here." He turned to Susan. "Ow."

"That shoulder's not good." Jake bent down.

He and Susan helped Blackie to his feet.

"Are the Apaches gone?" Blackie asked.

"Yes, but they left a few reminders." Jake took hold of his good arm.

Susan still held the towel on his chest while they slowly walked toward the boarding house.

Two days later, Blackie sat up in bed with his left arm in a sling. Susan Blackhawk walked in with a tray of food. "Ahhh . . . are those flapjacks I smell? I'm starvin'."

She nodded, smiled, and set the tray in his lap. "You've been sleeping."

"This is great. A beautiful woman, a plateful of good food. What else could a man want?"

Susan blushed, cast her eyes downward.

Blackie grinned. "Come now, you must know how beautiful you are."

"Cheyenne men do not know such a word.'

"So, how do they make you know how much you're wanted?"

She sat on the edge of the bed. "How many horses a warrior offered was what he thought of the woman."

"Was that for marriage?"

"Yes, but before that—sometimes the woman would start the courtship by looks, words, hand signals."

"And what would the man do?"

"Well, the young girl or her family would continue or they could refuse the man.

He sometimes would sit around, make funny faces, and play the flute."

"I couldn't play a flute."

She grinned. "But, you could look funny."

Blackie stuffed his mouth full of flapjacks and puffed out his cheeks.

"See—you did it." She laughed.

He screwed up his face again, then swallowed his mouthful. "You *are* beautiful."

Susan blushed again. "And you are a good man."

"Thank you." He gently stroked her left shoulder.

She relaxed to his touch and slumped back into his good arm. Blackie squeezed her close and kissed her neck.

Her eyes widened for a moment. *She did not know a kiss, but his lips felt soft and warm on her neck.*

He lingered, turned her head toward his face. She gazed into his dark eyes and saw the fire of his passion. He touched his lips to her forehead, down the tip of her nose to her perfect-fitted lips, and pressed tenderly against them. Susan shivered when she felt the pressure on her lips, but relaxed when he opened his mouth and spread his warm moisture to her.

"Oh . . ." She pulled back. "It makes me breathless."

"Good—it's supposed to."

"I have never been like this with a man."

"Not even the Apache chief?"

"No. He is very strong and manly, but we have not yet been close."

Blackie marveled at her. "I'm flattered that you're with me."

"You don't offer horses, but you move me." She watched his eyes.

He pulled her close again. This time, his lips sought her open mouth and pressed hard against her. They rolled together onto the food tray for a moment before Blackie pushed it off the bed. He winced from the pain in his bad shoulder.

"Are you not hungry now?" she asked.

"Very much so—for you." He caressed her shoulders and moved his hands down to her waist in a slow deliberate way.

She tingled as he kissed her again—longer this time and more passionate. Sensations coursed through her she had never known as his hands explored her breasts.

Their gasps came quicker now until they groped at each other's clothes. Pulling, tugging, they started removing restrictive clothing for physical freedom. Halfway through the exploration, a sudden noise shattered their bliss.

The door opened. Jake burst in. "Blackie—we better get down to the stable. Oops!"

CHAPTER TWENTY ONE

Jake stepped back into the doorway. He flushed. "Sorry."

Susan Blackhawk quickly slid off the bed and adjusted her clothes.

Blackie sat up straight against the headboard. "It's all right, Jake. Something wrong at the stable?"

"No. I just thought it was time to go after Jessica. That is, if your arm's healed enough?" Jake poked his head around the door jam.

"My arm's better. Susan here, has been a good nurse."

Jake grinned. "Yeah, I can see that."

"I better go." Susan did not look at Jake and walked past him.

"It just happened," Blackie said.

"She's a beautiful girl." Jake grabbed a chair and sat down.

"That she is. I think I'll be ready in the morning."

"Good. I'll outfit the horses. Is the girl going with us?"

Blackie scratched his head. "Might be a good idea."

* * * *

Maco's great pinto stallion strode easily into the Apache stronghold with Maco and Jessica upon its back. She clung tightly to the mighty warrior. *What now? This was the third time he'd captured her. Were they lovers? He had her once. She wanted it too.*

Surely he'd want her again. Would she respond again? What about Jake? The big paint slowed as they approached the camp.

White Horse was the first one to meet them. "So, you bring the white woman again as your spoils."

"It was she I went for." Maco dismounted, helped Jessica down.

"I thought we would burn the whole town, scalp all the whites."

"Porico, my brother, we made our raid—swift and sure—no Apaches killed. It was just. I got what I wanted."

White Horse's voice rose. "You got what you wanted! That is not the Apache way. What did the band get? We are one."

"There will be other raids. More gold to reap. Be patient."

"This woman is a curse." White Horse pointed to Jessica and stormed off.

Jessica looked after him, then at Maco. "Why do you want me? Your tribe does not."

"Did you not . . ." he started in Apache, then switched to Spanish, "know—when we were together?"

Jessica watched him. The warrior's face changed from fierce to settled. "Yes, I know. I felt it, too."

"Then it shall happen again. And no more escapes. You will be part of this tribe."

"Are you taking me as a wife?"

"We shall see. Now go to my wickiup." He motioned.

Jessica backed away from him, turned, and walked toward his wickiup.

Maco watched her leave, then guided his pony to the other tethered horses.

Alone in the wickiup, Jessica sat on the fur close to the fire pit. She folded her arms and stared at the entrance. *Soon he would come for her. She felt the anticipating trembles, the quivers up and down her body. Would his savage lovemaking take her beyond the limits of a white woman? Somehow she didn't think white or red—just man and woman. This must be the way God meant it to be.* A cold shiver ran through her. She found a stick and poked at the embers.

Maco rubbed his pinto down and turned him loose with the other horses in the small enclosure. He stood staring at the afternoon sun's shadows moving over the canyon's rocks. *Soon twilight would come, then darkness. He would lay with the beautiful white woman again. She had shown him a passion not experienced with an Apache woman. What would he do with her? Take her as a wife or kill her when finished with her?* He blinked the glaze from his eyes and listened to the gentle wind rustle through the trees. *He must go higher up into the trees and rocks to decide what to do.*

Maco's paint lifted his head, stuck his nose into the air. He pawed the ground, whinnied, and shifted back and forth. The other horses moved about nervously.

Maco looked around, did not smell anything, and started upward through the rocks. He had not gone very far before a grizzly charged out of the trees. Maco turned too late and the bear ripped a huge claw at his shoulder, tore a chunk of skin away. The Apache tumbled to the ground. The bear swung around, charged again. This time its jaws chomped at Maco's head, but the warrior ducked and bolted to his feet. He ran to a nearby tree and climbed upward. The grizzly followed, growling, clawed at Maco's legs. He settled on a high branch, pulled out his knife, and slashed at the bear's paws. The bear lunged at him and dug a claw into his leg, but Maco cut the top of its paw with several

quick gashes, drawing blood. The bear recoiled. Maco pulled off his war band and wrapped it around his left leg. The bleeding did not stop and the bear lunged again, biting Maco's left foot. He jerked backward, freeing his foot, but more blood spilled from the wound. The grizzly's growls grew louder and Maco's grunts echoed throughout the canyon.

White Horse, sitting beside the campfire, heard the battle sounds and grabbed his rifle. He motioned to two braves to follow him and ran toward the cries.

When they approached the battleground, White Horse stopped and signaled the other warriors to circle behind. He cocked his rifle, crept close, and put the bear in his sights. Blood poured from Maco's wounds onto the bear's head. The bear roared, thrust his claws at Maco. White Horse squeezed his rifle's trigger and the grizzly fell to the ground. The other braves rushed to the bear's carcass, poked at it with their lances. The bear did not move.

"Maco, are you all right?" White Horse started up the tree.

"Porico, you are truly my brother. I owe you my life." Maco slumped forward.

White Horse caught him. "We will get you down. You have lost much blood."

The other two warriors helped take Maco from the tree. He lost consciousness from so much loss of blood.

"We must get him to the Medicine Man or he will die." White Horse stared at his still brother.

After they carried Maco to his wickiup, one of the braves summoned the Medicine Man.

Jessica gasped when she saw Maco. "Is he dead?"

White Horse kneeled beside his brother. "He is not yet astride the Great Mustang in Usen's tribe."

She dipped a cloth in water and patted his forehead. "He's hardly breathing."

"Do not disturb his spirit." White Horse stood.

Jessica looked up at him. "I'm trying to help him."

"The shaman will be here soon."

"He's still bleeding." She dabbed at his wounds.

The entrance flap opened; a short man wearing a kilt, a black mask, and a tall wooden-slat headdress entered the wickiup. His body was painted and he carried a wooden sword. He gazed at Maco, then began singing and shaking two rattles. He danced around Maco and Jessica, then waved her away. After a few minutes, the shaman stopped, took an herbal substance out of a pouch, and applied it to Maco's wounds.

Jessica watched the fierce-looking man administer to Maco. "I only hope he knows what he's doing."

"Our medicine is powerful," White Horse said, "but, the white man brought invisible diseases that were more deadly."

"What has put Maco down is not invisible. It was a grizzly bear."

"Then he will be saved."

The Medicine Man started dancing around Maco again. He shook his sword and rattles in the air and chanted his spirit song.

"How long will he do this?" Jessica asked.

White Horse sat down near the entrance. "Until Maco is healed."

"I will wait also." She moved back against the lodge wall.

When darkness started to swallow the daylight, White Horse built a fire in the fire pit. The shaman, sweaty from his vigorous dance, bent to Maco's shallow breathing. Jessica moved closer to Maco, but the Medicine Man waved her back with his sword. She strained to hear his breaths.

White Horse stood over her. "It is time for food. Come."

"No. I will stay with Maco until . . ." She held back her tears.

White Horse mellowed toward her. "You—good woman."

Jessica did not respond. She stared at Maco's still body.

The shaman continued his ritual until after Jessica had fallen asleep. White Horse also was asleep by the entrance. Maco stirred, opened his eyes to dancing shadows on the walls. He groaned enough so the Medicine Man crouched beside him and waved a rattle over his head. Maco saw who it was and tried to rise up. The shaman shook his head and kept him down.

"I must get up." Maco twisted his body.

Jessica heard him and roused out of a restless sleep. "Maco." She crawled to him, put his head in her lap.

He gazed into her face; a slight smile crossed his lips.

"You will be all right." She brushed back his hair.

The Medicine Man saw the bleeding had stopped under the herb pack on his left leg and foot. He waved his sword over Maco's body and walked out of the wickiup.

Jessica caressed Maco's forehead and rocked him in her arms.

White Horse awakened, stood over him with a wide grin on his face. "Brother, the spirits are good to you."

"Porico, you saved me." Maco's tone was stronger. "I will never forget."

"I'll get you some food." Jessica lowered his head to the fur and went outside.

White Horse bent down. "The white one is a good woman. She could be Apache."

Maco looked surprised. "You said she was a bad omen. What changed?"

"She would not leave you."

"And you would not also."

"But, I am Apache and your brother."

"That is good. I will heal now."

Jessica came back with a plate of corn and beans. She set it down next to Maco and raised his head into her lap. "Eat—you will regain your strength."

CHAPTER TWENTY TWO

Jake, Blackie, and Susan Blackhawk rode hard out of Adobe Crossing. Blackie's left arm was in a sling, but the pain had subsided quite a bit. He held Ace steady with his right hand.

Susan Blackhawk rode beside Blackie. *She felt close to him now. He had saved her life by taking an arrow. The Apaches were vicious like the Comanches who had captured her and killed her mother. Maco, the Apache, had taken her from the Comanches. He called the Apaches Nide—the people, but they were enemy. Yet, he was kind to her, a strong leader, and he aroused her. But so did Blackie, the White-Eyes. What would happen when they met in battle? She was half French, half Cheyenne. How could she choose between them? Americans and Mexicans squeezed the Apache and the Cheyenne nations. They had to fight for freedom. Blackie and Jake got caught in the middle. What would she do?* She glanced at Blackie. His eyes were fixed on the trail. She spurred her horse.

Jake quickened the pace by urging Sam's powerful strides forward. *He didn't know how they could rescue Jessica. The war chief could have killed them all when he took her. That was unlike an Apache raider. What was his game? Mutual respect? Bigger stakes? The Apache was a cunning killer. He killed out of honor and need. Who could blame him? His lands and the air he breathes were shrinking.* Jake adjusted his hat to keep the sun out of his eyes.

Blackie trailed Jake and Susan by a few paces. *His stallion could easily overtake the other two, but he wanted to guard their rear. He marveled how well Susan fit her horse. The Cheyenne were born for horseback. She was a real beauty and quite a woman. He had never known love, only women's charms. Now, his thoughts grew deeper for her. Would she respond?* He glanced up. The sun was past the noon high. *They would hit the Apache stronghold at dark.*

* * * *

Near dusk, the Apache encampment bustled with preparation for a feast celebrating Maco's recovery. The women roasted fresh deer meat over the large fire pit. The men put on ceremonial headdresses, brought out colorful shields laced with eagle feathers. They drove their lances, topped with scalps, into the earth in front of Maco's wickiup. The Medicine Man started the spirit dance with his chanting. Fierce warriors followed his lead and joined in, rotating in a wide circle around the fire.

Maco heard the chants and stirred. Jessica sat at his side ready to help. He motioned for her to open the entrance flap so he could see out. She stepped outside and pulled the flap back. The sparks of the fire shot upward. The dancers quickened their fury. Then she went back inside and helped Maco lift up.

"They dance for you," she said.

He smiled. "It is good to be Apache."

"Yes, I can see that." She touched his arm.

Before he could respond, a war cry rang out and a rifle's bullet explored in the chest of one of the dancing warriors. Arrows and bullets hailed into the area where the men and women gathered. They ran for cover, but several fell in their tracks, bleeding from the onslaught. With Jessica's help, Maco crawled to the opening. Riders in war paint raced back and forth through the camp.

"Comanches!" Maco backed away from the entrance. "My rifle—my lance!"

Jessica reached out, pulled the flap shut. "You cannot go out there. Your leg—your foot—You can't walk."

"My people need me. It is an honor to die for them."

She held him. "I won't let you go."

"They have come for Susan Blackhawk. I stole her from them, but they stole her from the Cheyenne." He struggled with her, but was too weak to loosen her grip.

"I can shoot. I'll get your rifle. They will not get to you." She bolted for the weapon.

112

"My lance—throw me my lance."

Jessica grabbed it and the rifle. Maco took the lance, edged back to the entrance. Jessica stuck the rifle through the opening and shot a Comanche leaning from his horse with a war hatchet raised. The brave fell.

White Horse and the other Apaches warriors scattered and armed themselves with their rifles and lances, but the Comanches kept attacking from all sides. They killed several Apaches, both men and women. Their dying cries echoed throughout the canyon, drove the warriors to fight harder.

Jake, Blackie, and Susan Blackhawk heard the battle at the canyon's entrance.

"Come on!" Jake spurred Sam to a gallop.

Blackie and Susan followed.

"Make some noise—holler." Jake rode hard, shot his gun into the air.

"Aieee!" Susan screamed.

Blackie thundered past her. "Stay behind me until we see what we're up against."

He and Jake rode into the camp guns blazing. The Comanches, taken by surprise, halted their attack, and turned to face the two intruders.

Susan saw them. "Comanches—they are after me."

"Well, they're not getting you." Jake pumped lead into the nearest Comanche.

Blackie shot two of the attackers as they stormed toward him. Jake's gun spit out fire at any threatening enemy until they backed off and rode for the cover of the rocks.

Jessica saw them. "Jake—over here." She waved Maco's rifle.

The three stopped at Maco's wickiup and dismounted.

"What happened?" Jake saw Maco lying on the ground.

"Maco was mauled by a grizzly. Then the Comanches came out of nowhere." She motioned them into the wickiup.

"They thought I was here," Susan Blackhawk said.

Jessica glanced at her. "Yes, I know."

"How is Maco?"

"He was in great pain. The Medicine Man administered to him." Jessica shifted her gaze to the war chief.

Susan knelt beside him. "He is a strong man."

Jake peered out the entrance. "The Comanches will attack again."

Maco raised up with his lance. "I must fight."

Jessica held him down. "No—you are too weak."

"A warrior must kill if there is danger." Susan grabbed his lance. "Help him up."

Jessica pointed the rifle at her. "I said no."

"Whoa, there." Jake jumped between them. "She's right. An Apache must do what his heart says."

"I agree," Blackie said.

Maco struggled to rise. Jake and Blackie helped him.

On his feet, Maco peered outside the wickiup at his fallen band. "I will summon my brother, Porico. He and I will lead the fight when the Comanches attack again."

"We'll help you." Jake stepped forward.

Blackie gripped his rifle. "Yeah, we'll help."

Jessica and Susan stood back.

"You are not healed yet," Jessica said.

"No matter." Maco took his rifle from her. "I fight."

The Comanches swarmed the camp again. This time, riding through and spraying bullets and arrows everywhere. Maco raised his hand for everyone to stay inside until they rode back through. When he heard their horses coming, he signaled and he, Jake, and Blackie rushed outside firing. White Horse saw them and motioned his braves into action. They shot at the charging enemy, leaped on their backs swinging war clubs and knives. The Apaches' onslaught surprised the Comanches so much they galloped on out the canyon.

Maco gathered his warriors around him. "Go—see who lives."

"What about the White-Eyes?" White Horse asked.

Maco hesitated a moment. "They are friends now. Do nothing."

White Horse twisted his mouth. "They were enemy."

"No more. I have spoken." He handed his rifle to Jake.

Jake held it and helped Maco back inside his wickiup.

Everyone else went inside except White Horse. He turned away, waved to the other warriors. "Draw your knives. Our enemies' scalps will sit atop our lodge poles."

They scoured the battlefield for dead Comanches and took their prizes.

Jessica heard and saw them outside. "Must they do that?"

"It is our birthright." Maco said. "A warrior must show his kill."

"It just seems barbaric," she said.

Maco raised his right hand. "We do not put bounty on scalps like the Mexicans and some Americans do."

"That's true," Jake said. "The Mexicans offer up to three hundred dollars for an Apache scalp."

Maco turned. "We had to fight. We first came from the Far North to the plains and hunted buffalo. Then the Spaniards, Mexicans, Comanches, Whites intruded on our territory. We are born fighters. We had no choice for survival."

"Same thing happened to the Cheyenne," Susan Blackhawk said, "except it was other tribes and the Whites who tried to force us from our homeland."

Maco leaned back against a wall. "Are you back with us now?"

She was not ready for that question and could not look at him. "I—I am not sure. I have found another interest . . ."

Blackie shifted from one foot to the other.

Susan watched him, but he did not speak.

Maco glanced at both of them. "Has the big White-Eyes taken my place?"

"She has taken mine next to you." Susan pointed at Jessica.

Jessica flushed, gazed into the fire. Jake looked at her and Maco. He gripped his rifle. Maco did not change his expression. The only sound came from the crackling fire.

Susan moved closer to Blackie. "We must go now."

"But, Jake . . ." Blackie stiffened.

"I'm ready. Seems things are settled here." He turned toward the entrance. "Is that right, Jessica?"

She rose, stood next to Maco. "I need to stay until he is well and strong again."

"Let's ride." Jake walked outside.

Blackie and Susan followed.

"I'll round up the horses," Blackie said.

Susan looked up at Jake. "There is something compelling about the Apache."

"Apparently." Jake adjusted his hat.

Blackie came back with their horses. They mounted and started out of the stronghold.

White Horse watched them go, then summoned his braves. "They are still enemy."

He and the other Apaches climbed on their ponies and rode out behind Jake, Blackie, and Susan Blackhawk. Far enough behind as to not be seen.

CHAPTER TWENTY THREE

The three riders rode in silence. White Horse and his men followed far enough behind so they were not seen, but could follow the tracks in the dark.

Jake never looked back. *He admired Jessica's grit for wanting to stay with Maco until he was healed, but wondered if it was more than that. The Apache seemed to have a savage magnetism that some women would be attracted to. But she was drawn to him the time they kissed. He would have to bide his time for now.* Up ahead, he saw a good spot close to the river. He motioned to Blackie. "We'll make camp there."

They reined up, tethered their horses to nearby trees. Jake and Blackie gathered some wood and started a fire. Susan unpacked a can of beans, warmed them, and made a pot of coffee. They rested against their saddles and ate.

The night was still except for the running water of the river. Blackie propped his head on his saddle and pulled a blanket up to his shoulders. Jake sat staring into the fire. Susan washed the utensils in the river. Walking back to camp, she heard a bird call that did not sound true. She listened again. This time, more acutely. Something was not right.

She hurried back to camp and started kicking dirt on the fire.

Jake jerked up. "What's wrong?"

"A killing party." She put her finger to her mouth.

"Comanches?"

"Or Apaches."

Jake drew his gun, shook Blackie.

Blackie threw his blanket off. "What . . .?"

"Indians." Jake crouched beside his saddle.

"Get down." Blackie waved at Susan.

An arrow flew past her head, hit a tree. She dove for cover. Jake tossed her a rifle. The large, orange full moon started its rise in the sky. Shadows crisscrossed around them in the trees.

Jake shot his rifle and dropped one of the shadows. War cries shattered the night now; bullets and arrows rained on them. Blackie and Jake returned the fire as fast as they could. Susan hugged the ground, but shot back at the raiders.

"How many?" Blackie asked

"About a dozen." Jake kept firing.

White Horse stayed back in the trees until his warriors had pinned the three down. He drew his knife and crept toward Jake who had backed against a tree. Jake shot two or three Apaches before he ran out of bullets and had to reload. White Horse saw his chance and lunged at Jake. His knife plunged into Jake's left shoulder blade knocking him to the ground. White Horse jumped on him like a big cat, pushed his face into the dirt. Jake bucked, threw the Apache off and drew his own knife. They rolled over and over, each with his knife aimed at the other's chest.

Blackie and Susan were too busy fending off the other warriors to help. They shot at shadows, hitting some, missing some.

After a bloody struggle, Jake, weakened by his wound, rolled on top and drove his knife into White Horse's chest. His wide-open eyes blinked once, then closed. Jake slumped off him, took a deep breath.

Blackie moved next to him, fired shots at a charging Apache. The other warriors saw White Horse did not move. They moved back into the trees where their horses were tied and mulled over what to do. After a few minutes, they climbed on their ponies and rode off.

Jake cautioned Blackie and Susan to stay put until he looked around.

"They're gone." Jake returned to camp.

"That's that," Blackie said.

"I don't know. When they tell Maco that I killed White Horse, he's not gonna be happy."

"Jake's right," Susan said. "An Apache must avenge his brother's death."

"Then we better hightail it to town." Jake tugged at his gunbelt.

* * * *

It was near first light when the Apache warriors reached their stronghold. They rode straight to Maco's wickiup and burst inside.

"Maco! Maco!"

The Apache leader jerked awake. "What? Who?"

"The tall White-Eyes has killed White Horse."

"Porico, my brother, is dead?"

"Yes, we trailed the two men and woman to their camp. White Horse said they were still enemy. He would not stop."

Maco sat up. "You attacked them?"

"Yes. They had killed our people."

"I told Porico they were friends now."

"They are friends no more. They killed White Horse."

Color drained from Maco's face. "Did you bring his body?"

"No. We could not recover him."

"I must go—bring my brother home. Bury him the Apache way."

"We will show you where."

Maco held out his arms. "Help me up."

"Are you able to ride?"

"I will ride for my brother. When I return and send Porico to Usen's tribe, war paint will cover my face again. My vengeance will not cease this time against the White-Eyes."

"Aieee, that is the Apache way."

Jessica, awake now on the other side of the wickiup, heard their plans. She shuddered. *Maco was not healed for a war party. Couldn't let him kill Jake. She had to warn him. How could she get away? She better not try to stop Maco now. She'd go after they left.* She closed her eyes, pretended to be asleep.

119

The warriors helped Maco onto his horse and the small band rode out of the camp. Jessica got up, looked outside, saw no one was near her wickiup. She darted out to the tethered horses, threw the saddle on her horse, and galloped away.

The Comanche raiding party, that had attacked the Apache stronghold and had been driven off, regrouped and saw Maco and his braves ride toward the river. They started out of the hills when Jessica rode close to their outlook.

The leader halted his braves. "She is white. We will take her. Do not kill."

The hostile raiders swooped down on Jessica. She saw them out of the corner of her left eye and kicked her horse in its sides. The horse took off with the Comanches in hot pursuit.

After a half-mile chase, Jessica's horse stumbled and threw her. She landed on her right shoulder, but ducked her head and rolled. Groggy and stunned, she shook the webs out of her head and lay still.

The Comanches surrounded her on their ponies; the leader dismounted and approached. He trained his rifle on her head when he saw she had a sidearm, then poked her with the rifle. She stirred, turned over. The Indians stared at her.

"What—what do you want with me?"

The leader waved her off. He did not understand her. He motioned her to rise. Slowly she did. Another brave brought her horse. After brushing off her clothes, she mounted. The Comanches rode in front and in back of her. Still stunned, she went along with them.

* * * *

Jake reined up at the sheriff's office in Adobe Crossing. The sun, straight up, ducked in and out of a few clouds. Blackie and Susan Blackhawk followed Jake into the office. After gathering more ammunition, they took their horses to the livery stable.

Construction had started the rebuilding of the town from the last Apache raid.

The three walked to the boarding house. Jake sent for the doctor to look at his arm.

After the doctor treated Jake's arm, they sat at the large table where the food was served.

"What are we doing about Jessica?" Blackie asked.

"We've got to go get her," Jake said.

Susan looked up. "She wanted to stay, care for Maco."

"That's right," Blackie said.

"Apaches do not forget." Susan drank from her water glass. "He will not let her go."

Jake blinked. "I know. We'll have to take her."

"He will come for us," Susan said. "You killed White Horse, his brother. He must avenge his death."

Jake took a swallow of coffee. "He said we were friends now."

"That is no longer true." Susan finished the last of her food and rose from the table.

"Are you going upstairs?" Blackie asked.

"Yes." She turned, walked toward the stairs.

Blackie looked at Jake. "Looks like we've got some problems."

"I'll have to think it out."

Blackie stood. "Gonna get some rest while I can." He walked out.

"Sure, go ahead." Jake stared blankly at the doorway.

Upstairs, Blackie started to walk past Susan's room, but stopped and pondered a minute. Then he knocked on her door. She opened it. Blackie stepped in, took her in his arms, and kissed her. She responded to him by pressing her warm body close to him. He caressed down her neck and shoulders to her breasts. His tongue darted into her moist mouth and swirled. She did not know this sensation, but felt it throughout her whole body and wrapped her arms around his neck, as her hunger flamed brighter. He roamed slowly over her succulent body inching her clothes off. Still entwined, he slid his clothes off and pressed his swollen staff between her legs. She moaned and he edged her to the bed where he entered her very slowly. Their bodies rocked gently until the heat became unbearable and the waves of their innermost juices exploded together.

* * * *

Maco's warriors led him to the river where White Horse's body lay in the sand. Maco jumped off his pony, took his brother in his arms. He looked skyward and wailed. "I will not forget you Porico. Your death will be avenged. You will ride the Great Mustang in Usen's sky. You will ride home on my horse."

The other braves put the dead Apaches on horses and started back to the stronghold.

A few miles on the trail, scouts who had been sent out earlier met Maco's group and reported Jessica had be taken captive by the Comanches.

Maco halted and listened to the scouts. "We must get her back."

"First, we have to bury our dead," one of the braves said. "Then, what about the White-Eyes? He killed White Horse."

Maco put a hand on his brother's back, laid behind his saddle. "You are right.

We must bury the dead the Apache way. We go." He pressed his knees against his pony's sides.

At the stronghold, wives and relatives of the dead met the Apaches. The wives wailed, cut their hair and arms, and scratched their faces in mourning. The dead warriors were buried in secret places and covered with rocks and dirt to keep animals away.

Maco stood in front of his brother's hidden cave. "We do not speak of the dead again, but I will never forget you, Porico."

At the council fire, Maco spoke to the men of the tribe. "The white woman has been captured by the Comanche enemy. She nursed me back to good health. She is friend. I must free her."

122

"The White-Eyes killed White Horse." A young brave stood up. "We must scalp him first."

Maco turned, hesitated a moment. "You are right. The Comanches will not kill her so soon. They will try to trade her for the Cheyenne woman I took from them. We will go after the White-Eyes. A white flag will catch the town off guard. We strike at dawn in two days."

CHAPTER TWENTY FOUR

Jessica lay by the fire tied to a large log. The Comanche camp was hidden in the mountains at the end of a long arroyo. The leader and other braves sat around the fire eating the cooked deer meat, grinning and staring at the white beauty. The tribe's women left the area after fixing the food. Young warriors pointed to each other excluding the older braves to determine who would have her first. The leader, a muscular Comanche with many scalps strapped to his pony, stood above the others. He pounded his chest several times declaring the woman was his. He was the same warrior who had killed Susan Blackhawk's mother during the raid on the Cheyenne village and carried Susan away many moons ago. After he had his fill of Jessica, he would trade her for the return of the pretty Cheyenne.

* * * *

Blackie and Susan Blackhawk lay in each other's arms savoring the fulfillment of their lovemaking. Contentment flowed in both bodies and they soon fell asleep.

When they awoke, it was dark and they went downstairs for food. After a good meal, they returned to Susan's room and made love again. This time, again falling asleep in each other's arms.

Susan awakened just before dawn the next day and looked out the window as light filtered through the last threads of the night. Lantern lights sprinkled around the town and morning movements broke out. The morning light spread as she gazed up and down the main street. *Was that horses she heard? Not galloping or trotting—just walking. A group of horses—this early.* Her eyes adjusted; she peered more closely at each end of the street. From the west end of town, several Apache ponies with riders walked down the street. Maco, the leader, held a white flag in his right hand. Susan jerked away from the window, hurried to the bed.

"Wake up—quick!" She shook Blackie.

"What? What is it?" He rubbed his eyes.

"Come look in the street."

Blackie crawled out of bed, ambled to the window. "I'll be damned. It's the Apaches—with a white flag." He watched a few moments. The horsemen stopped. "Now what do you suppose . . .?"

"Something doesn't seem right," Susan said.

"Means they want to talk."

"It could be a trick." She took a closer look. "That's Maco."

"I better wake Jake." Blackie pulled on his pants and shirt, rushed out the door.

Susan dressed quickly, sat by the window. She held her pistol.

Jake and Blackie burst into the room.

"Here—look" Susan motioned to Jake.

"It is Maco and some of his warriors." He kneeled at the window.

"What do you suppose they want?" Blackie asked.

Susan sat back. "He wants Jake."

"Why?"

"He killed White Horse," Susan said.

Jake stood. "What's he got to trade."

"Jessica," Blackie said.

"I don't see her."

Susan moved away from the window. "They will take you back to their stronghold, then let her go."

"And what if they decide to keep us both?"

"That's the chance you take."

Blackie paced back and forth. "I don't like it. I'm going down there—have a powwow."

"Hold on." Jake adjusted his gunbelt. "If he wants me. I'm ready."

"I better go, too," Susan said.

Blackie stopped her. "No. Stay here. You may be right—it could be at trick."

Jake was already on the stairs when Blackie caught up with him. They checked their guns and walked out the front door.

Maco sat still on his pony, waited for the White-Eyes to come forward. *The white flag indicated a truce. Would they fall for it? The Apache must use whatever he can to defeat the white intruders. The big man killed his brother. He must die.* Maco narrowed his eyes as the two men walked slowly toward him and his raiding party.

"Watch their eyes and hands," Jake said to Blackie.

"Yeah. I learned that."

Jake shook his hands at his sides. Blackie put a hand on his gun.

Maco gripped his rifle tighter.

The two cultures waited for the other's move. Jake, hard-boned and wide-shouldered spread his arms out from his sides. Maco motioned with his rifle at the gesture. Jake and Blackie kept walking with their eyes focused on the Apache.

Back at the boarding house, Susan Blackhawk walked onto the porch and looked toward the other end of the street. Jake and Blackie stood in front of Maco and his warriors. She skipped down the steps and hurried toward Maco and the two men.

Maco shifted his eyes from the two men in front of him to the movement down the street. *It was her, the Cheyenne. He had taken her from the pool. She was a beautiful maiden—still should be a maiden. He hadn't touched her, though feelings inside told him to. She was not like other squaws he had known. Why had he chosen the white woman first? The Comanches wanted her back. A good trade.* A few seconds later, his attention leaped back to the two White-Eyes.

Jake watched Maco's eyes closely as they switched from place to place. Maco pointed his rifle at Susan Blackhawk. Jake turned, held up a hand for her to stop. She ignored his command, kept walking toward them.

Blackie stepped between her and Maco. "Why did you come here? I told you to stay put."

"You may need my help." She did not look at him, but kept her eyes on Maco.

Maco gestured to her. "The white man killed my brother. He must pay the Apache price."

"No. White Horse did not heed your word. We were friends. We helped you fight the Comanches."

"That is true. Still, Porico was my only brother."

"I know. I am sorry. But killing Jake won't bring back White Horse."

"His spirit will know I have avenged him." Maco raised his rifle upward.

"I cannot let that happen. You take me instead."

Jake understood her last remark. "No. I'll not allow it. If he wants me, we'll fight the Apache way. Whoever wins, wins."

"It would be with knives," she said. "A fight to the finish. One of you would die."

"Tell him." He put a hand on his Bowie knife.

Maco saw what he did and aimed his rifle at Jake.

"Wait." Susan waved her hands. "He said he would fight you alone."

"I could kill him now."

"You are not that cold."

"I am Apache—enemy. I take many scalps."

"True, but you are a great leader also."

"My warriors want revenge."

"It was your brother. You must fight the White-Eyes."

Maco shifted his weight on his pony. "It shall be."

The other warriors grumbled and they stirred their horses.

Maco raised his right hand with the rifle in it. "It is done."

The braves stopped.

"Should we do this here in the middle of town?" Jake asked.

Susan stepped between them. "That is not a good idea."

It was past first light now. Early dawn turned into a cloudless day with a slight warm breeze. The town stirred. Some residents left their houses and looked on with apprehension. The Apaches always cast a fearful net over the town. Maco's surprise raid had turned tame. He swung his mount around and headed out of town. Jake followed.

Blackie helped Susan up behind him on Ace. "Hope this works out."

"We may be in trouble either way. If Maco kills Jake, he will want me back and kill you. If Jake kills Maco, the other Apaches may not honor the victor's code and will kill all of us."

"Sounds like a death wish either way." Blackie tugged at the reins.

Maco stopped at a shallow dry arroyo a short ways out of town. The bottom was sandy and flat. He motioned for everyone to dismount, told his warriors to form a circle around him and the tall White-Eyes. Blackie and Susan stood off to one side.

Jake threw off his hat and unbuckled his gunbelt. He stood only slightly taller than the muscular Apache leader. They each had hunting knives at their sides and stared intently at each other. One of the braves motioned for them to stick their knives into the sand at the middle of the circle. He then raised his hand between them.

CHAPTER TWENTY FIVE

At the drop of the hand, Jake lunged for his Bowie knife, but Maco beat him, kicked it away and grabbed his own blade. He slashed at Jake's chest, but missed. Jake ducked at the next thrust at his head and rolled toward his Bowie in the sand. Snatching it, he came at Maco hard and cut his left arm above the elbow. Maco winced, retreated to his right, and set himself for another attack. Jake took a breath, focused on Maco's eyes, and circled the Apache. Blood from Maco's arm dripped onto the sand. He bent, picked up a clump, and threw it into Jake's eyes. Jake raised his hands, tried to dust the sand off, but Maco was on him in a second, knocked him to the ground and piled on. He jabbed with his knife, but Jake twisted away and grasped Maco's forehand below the knife. He gripped as tight as he could holding the knife away from his chest. Maco pressed with all his weight inching the knife closer to Jake's heart. Jake kicked his knee into Maco's back, jarred him. It was just enough for him to roll onto one of Maco's legs and twist away. He regained his feet, then rushed Maco. The sand still stung his eyes, but he managed to see better and he knocked Maco on the ground. Jake flattened him with a leap onto his chest. Maco wheezed; the air went out of him. Jake pinned his large knife against Maco's throat just enough to draw fresh blood. Maco relaxed and his knife slipped out of his hand.

"I should kill you," Jake said, "but I won't. I want Jessica back."

Maco's dilated eyes met his. "I do not have her."

"What?"

"The Comanches took her."

Jake still held Maco down. The mounted warriors closed in on him. Blackie reached for his gun. Susan backed away.

"Hold it!" Jake loosened his grip and rose to his feet.

Maco rubbed his throat and slowly sat up. He raised a hand to his braves. They stopped. "The White-Eyes could have killed me."

"Blackie, back off." Jake motioned.

Maco rose now and looked at the blood on his fingers. "You killed White Horse. Why did you not kill me?"

"White Horse surprise attacked us after you called us friends. He picked me. I had no choice." Jake placed his knife back in its sheath. "You and I had a fair fight. Enough blood has been shed."

"It seems we are destined to be blood brothers."

Jake eyed the surrounding Apaches. "We'll see."

"Sometimes Porico's hot blood ran too fast through his veins." Maco reached for his knife.

Jake stepped on it. "Are we done here?"

"You won. Should we not free the white woman?"

Jake pulled his foot off the knife. "You say the Comanches have her. How do you know that?"

Maco bent slowly, picked up his knife. "My scouts told me when we gathered our dead by the river."

"Where is their camp?"

"In the mountains between the river and our stronghold."

Jake moved back a step. "Will we trust each other?"

"We must—for now. But who will the white woman choose?"

"We'll have to get her first—then she'll decide."

Maco looked at Susan Blackhawk. "The Comanches want that one back."

"Wait a minute." Blackie stepped forward. "We're not here to trade."

Susan took hold of his arm.

"He's right," Jake said. "No trades. "The Comanches are not to be trusted."

Maco called for his horse. "Then we ride. It will be dark when we get to their camp." He leaped on his mount and headed toward the mountains.

Jake, Blackie, and Susan followed a short distance behind. The Apaches loped along at a good pace into the middle of the afternoon. As the sun started down, Maco turned into the arroyo's entrance and slowed the horses to a trot. Dust from fast-moving horses could be seen at a great distance.

Jake took out his field glass and peered at the mountain ahead. No smoke. *They had not been seen.* He patted Sam's neck. "Good horse."

Maco raised a hand about half way up the arroyo. "We must split here. My men and I will go up on each side. You three ride straight up the arroyo. If they see you and attack, we'll close in from the sides."

"If they don't see us, how will we know where Jessica is?" Jake asked.

Maco's eyes narrowed. "If she is not dead, she will be with the leader. His will be the biggest lodge."

"I'll go in shooting."

"That is not wise. They will kill her first." Maco tightened his reins.

Jake kicked Sam's sides. "Let's go."

∗ ∗ ∗ ∗

Jessica twisted her arms, tried to ease the pain on her wrists from the rawhide tied to them. She had fallen in and out of dazed sleep since her capture. No Comanche had approached her yet. *She knew they would come—only a matter of time. And Maco—would he miss her when he got back to camp after retrieving White Horse's body? Dusk was coming. She was hungry.* She glanced around the campfire area. Only one Comanche stood guard. The women had not yet started their evening food. She tugged at her bonds, but they cinched tighter. Sinking backward, she waited.

A short time later, the women came out of their lodges and started making supper. Jessica smelled meat cooking. It made her mouth water. The fire grew brighter and sent sparks into the gathering darkness.

133

The Comanche leader pushed open the flap of his lodge and walked toward Jessica. He took his knife and cut her arms free from the branches. With rawhide still streaming from her wrists, he pulled her into his lodge. Many scalps hung from his lodge pole. She shuddered when she saw them. He pointed to a buffalo robe lying beside the fire pit. She sat down on it and stared up at him. His muscles glistened in the firelight. His chest was hairless and his hair long and black. He loosened his breeches and exposed himself to her. She shied away, unable to bear the sight of his swollen manhood. Crouching, he ripped the buttons loose on her shirt. She jerked backward, but her breasts fell free. She crisscrossed her arms over her breasts, all the time watching his eyes explore her. When he tugged at her riding pants, she sent her right foot hard to his groin. The big Comanche fell backward, but had one pants leg torn off. She turned over, tried to jump away from him. Dazed, he shook his head and grabbed at her other leg. Jessica kicked at his face with her free leg, but it did not stop him. He clawed at her underpants ripping them off. Pinning her down on her back he piled on top of her as she cried out and tried to squirm away. His weight was too much. She sank under it and waited. Just as he started to thrust into her, the lodge's entrance flap burst open. Jake Harwood leaped on the Comanche's back and plunged his Bowie knife into him.

"Jake!" Jessica pulled the buffalo robe around her.

He rolled the Indian off her legs and pulled out his knife. "You all right?"

"Yes, thanks to you. How did . . .?"

"We got lucky. Caught 'em by surprise."

"We?"

"Yeah—Blackie, Susan Blackhawk, and some of the Apaches."

"The Apaches—Maco?"

"He showed the way to this camp."

"I'm glad you found it—and me, in time. Thank you."

"Better get dressed. We gotta get out of here."

She started to stand. "All right."

He looked at her. "I'll wait outside."

"Jake—I'm glad it's you."

"Glad you're not harmed." He walked out.

Gunfire erupted around the camp now. The surprise was broken. Apaches and Comanches fought with guns, bows, and lances; the Apaches mounted on horses had the upper hand.

Maco fought his way to Jake just as Jessica came out of the leader's lodge. "I see you found her."

"Yeah, you guessed right when you told me where she'd be." Jake drew his gun, scanned the fight.

Jessica tucked her shirt in, shook her ruffled hair.

"Was she harmed?" Maco asked.

She looked up to Maco. "No. Thanks to Jake, he got there just in time."

"That is good." Maco dismounted. "The Comanche scalp is yours." He pointed to Jake.

Jake drew back. "I don't take scalps."

"Then I take it." Maco drew his knife. "She was mine when they took her."

Jessica stepped in front of him. "I'm not anybody's."

Maco saw the fire in her eyes, backed off. "It is our way."

"Just a minute." Jake blocked his way also. "We don't own anyone."

Maco pondered a moment. "What about the black people?"

"How do you know about them?"

"We have heard from the black soldiers."

Jake moved back. "You're right. Some Americans do own slaves, but that's in a different part of the country. Out here, every man is free."

"Except the Apache and other tribes who are hunted by the Mexicans." Maco's face twisted. He waved his rifle in the air, let out a war cry.

His warriors had overrun the camp and were scalping their enemies. Blackie and Susan Blackhawk rode up.

"We're about done here, Jake," Blackie said.

"You're right. We got what we came for."

Susan looked Jessica over. "She is not Comanche now?"

"No, I'm not. They held you captive once, too, didn't they?"

Maco stepped between them. "There is still a larger Comanche force. It may come back at any time."

"He's right," Jake said. "Time to vamoose."

Maco motioned to Jessica. "Ride behind me on my pony."

She studied him, then Jake. "I'm going with Jake."

Jake took her arm and led her to his horse.

Maco narrowed his eyes and stared after them. *We are not done.*

CHAPTER TWENTY SIX

Back in Adobe Crossing, Jessica took off her dirty clothes and stepped into a tub of foamy hot water. She propped her head against the rim and bent her knees as she sank into the soothing water. "Ahhh . . ." Her aches and pains seemed to disappear as she splashed.

"Heaven . . ."

Soon, her eyes fluttered and closed. She drifted into a watery dreamland. *She chose Jake over Maco. He saved her from the Comanche's attempted rape. But she and Maco had made love. An impromptu exciting tryst. She liked it, but he was Apache; she was from New Orleans. Jake had saved her from the Apaches who ambushed her stagecoach. Were those raiders Maco's?* Jessica stirred. The pain of that massacre jerked her awake. Her sleepy eyes slowly focused and she cupped water on her face. Now, fully awake, she relaxed again.

There was no knock, but the bathroom door opened. Jake Harwood walked in. "Oops! Looks like I'm always walking in on somebody."

"You're right about that—it's my body." She gave him a big grin.

He gawked at her. "I see."

"Guess I should've locked the door."

"Just needed a shave." He rubbed his stubble.

"Well, don't just stand there—use the wash basin and the mirror."

"But you're . . ."

"I'm sure you've seen a naked woman before."

"Yeah, but—but—not as pretty as you."

She blushed now. "Why thank you, Jake."

He walked past her with shaving mug, soap, razor, and brush in hand. She followed him with her eyes. He did not look at her until the mirror reflected her image. Stealing a quick glance of her, he poured water into the basin and lathered the soap in the mug.

"Shouldn't you take your shirt off?" she asked.

He stopped stirring. "Guess I should." He set the mug down and pulled off his shirt.

"That's better." She admired his rippling back muscles.

"Glad you like it." He smeared soap over his beard, brushed it in.

"So, tell me—who else did you walk in on?"

He stopped shaving. "I don't know if they'd want me to say."

"They? You mean a couple?"

He paused. "I don't know about this."

"Come on, Jake." She coaxed him.

Half his face was clean; half was soaped up. "Remember your old friend, Blackie."

"Blackie? You walked in on Blackie—and who?"

"The Cheyenne—Susan Blackhawk."

She shifted in the tub, lifted up. "You caught them in a compromising position?"

"Yep." He stared at her breasts.

"Good for Blackie. He finally found a good woman."

"Didn't think you two hit it off."

"She was in Maco's wickiup when he brought me in. I don't think she liked that."

"Probably not if she was his woman."

"From what I saw, she wasn't his woman."

"Were you?"

Jessica sank lower in the water. "How about getting some more hot water for me?"

"Are you ignoring my question?"

"No. The water's getting colder."

He sought her eyes, but she turned. "I'll go down and bring you some more water."

She sighed after he left. *Should she tell him what happened? Or should she wait? Both men moved her, but Maco was part of her now. Jake has seen her naked, but he hasn't approached her yet.*

Jake came back with a bucket of hot water. "Better move your feet." He poured the water into the tub.

She stirred it around until the water warmed.

He walked back to the mirror, picked up his razor. "Now, are you going to answer my question?" He stroked the razor down the right side of his face.

"No."

"No? Does that mean, no you're not going to answer me or no you weren't his woman?"

She turned her head so he could not see her face. "It means no, I wasn't." *She didn't lie much, but she had to here.* Then she splashed water on her face.

He finished shaving, rinsed his face, and dried with a towel. "'Bout spent all the time I can around here."

"You mean you're going on to California?"

"Yep. What about you? You and Blackie still want to settle here?"

"Don't know. He's kinda tied up with Susan now."

"I gathered that."

"You still want company?"

"Didn't want any at first, but you—yeah."

"Then, I think I'll go with you."

"Can you be ready tomorrow?"

She half rose from the tub. "I'm almost ready right now."

He gawked at her inviting body. "We better wait on that."

"Silly," she laughed, "I meant ready to leave for California."

He grinned. "Yeah—sure."

CHAPTER TWENTY SEVEN

Maco and his men returned to their stronghold. The women, children, and elders saw the Comanche scalps, but no White-Eyes scalps. They started to dance and chant.

The Medicine Man approached, held up his hand. The dancing stopped. "Bad omen. No white scalps. Evil spirits replace the White-Eyes." He broke into a spirit dance, emitting eerie sounds.

Maco stood beside his wickiup, watched the Medicine Man whirl and twirl against the evil spirits. *He believed Usen understood why he let the white men live. He needed their help. He would go off alone in the desert, pray and stay until he received guidance.*

While Maco was gone, a group of Mexicans raided the camp, killed some warriors, many elders, and carried off women and children. They also stole good horses. Two days later, an outbreak of cholera hit the stronghold. Half the remaining tribe came down with the disease. The weak died; the strong lingered. The Medicine Man danced around the camp, blamed the white man.

When Maco returned, the Medicine Man halted him. "Evil spirits tell the truth. Look what happened. A Mexican death raid and disease."

Maco saw all the death and anguish. He called on the Medicine Man to heal the sick and gathered the six strongest warriors in his wickiup. "We will raid the Mexicans, get our people back."

"We need more rest," one of the braves said, "to get our strength back."

Maco looked around the wickiup, saw the strained expressions of their faces. "All right. In two days, we ride."

$$* * * *$$

Jake knocked on Blackie's door.

"Who's there?" Blackie slowly opened the door. "Jake."

"Jessica and I are wanting to head out for California. What about you and Susan?"

Blackie pulled the door wide open. "Come in. I'm ready. Not much left of Adobe Crossing. Like the idea of the Gold Country. I'll go with you to Susan's room."

Down the hall, they knocked on Susan Blackhawk's door.

She opened it without asking who was there. "Jake— Blackie. Come in."

"Susan," Blackie said, "Jake's set on going to California. How about you?"

"Are you and Jessica going?"

"Yeah."

"I don't know. I thought you and I might return to my people. The Cheyenne are being squeezed like the Apache and other tribes. The white man is relentless."

Blackie scratched his chin. "I'm white and you're half French and beautiful. We two can't stop the migration west."

"I know. I am afraid, but if you want me to go, then I go."

Blackie gave her a hug. "Good."

Jake moved toward the door. "After we get outfitted, we'll leave tomorrow."

Early the next morning, the two men and two women checked their supplies and rode west out of Adobe Crossing toward California.

After a day and a half on the trail, Jake halted and took out his field glass. A cloud of dust rose in the distance. "That dust is moving this way fast. Better pull off the trail, wait and see." He led them to a group of trees.

About a half-hour later, Maco and his six armed warriors, with war paint and war bands, galloped into view. Jake motioned everyone to stay put and rode out of the trees.

Maco saw him, halted his men.

"You are painted for war again," Jake said.

"The Mexicans forced a war. They raided our camp; killed many of The People, took our women, children, horses."

"So you ride."

"We must get them back."

Jake moved his right hand away from his chest. "Do you need some help?"

"It is not your fight." Maco extended his rifle.

"We have fought together before."

Maco focused on Jake's eyes. "Our Medicine Man told us you caused evil spirits to descend on us. The fever—the Mexicans."

"You mean cholera?"

"Bad death."

"It is."

Maco relaxed. "If you help us, the evil spirits may go away."

"We're on our way to California. Let's see what my companions say?" He rode back into the trees.

Blackie emerged first. "What's going on with them?"

"They're on a raiding party to Mexico. The Mexicans killed many Apaches, stole women and children—horses."

"They want our help?"

"Yeah."

"What if they turn on us?" Blackie asked.

"I don't think they will."

"What about Jessica and Susan?"

"We'll ask them." Jake rode to them.

Jessica and Susan held their horses.

"Well—what about it?" Jake asked. "Want to help out Maco?"

Jessica nodded yes. Susan shook her head.

"Susan—why?" Jake moved near her.

"The Mexicans are allies with the Comanches—Comancheros. Very dangerous."

"Then you and Blackie stay behind."

Blackie moved in. "Wait a minute. I don't want to miss a good fight."

"We can't leave Susan alone." Jake turned his stallion.

Susan held up a hand. "If Blackie goes—I go."

Maco raised his rifle into the air. "Good. The Mexicans will pay with many scalps."

"All right," Jake said. "Let's head out. But how do you know which way they went?"

"They come from Chihuahua. It is a long ride from here—through deserts, valleys between mountains to the Casas Grandes river." Maco pointed south. "A good five days."

Jake swung alongside Maco. "You lead. Just make sure your braves know we're with you."

"My warriors want the Mexicans."

"Then let's go get 'em. There's about four hours daylight left today." Jake spurred Sam.

That evening as darkness swallowed the land, they camped by a small river. The Apaches made a smokeless fire. Jake and the others picketed their horses, then pulled the saddles and blankets off. Maco positioned two warriors outside the camp as guards. Jake dropped his saddle close to Jessica's near the fire. Blackie and Susan Blackhawk's saddles were plopped a few feet away. The Apaches threw blankets on the soft earth close to the river. They ate dried mule meat and bedded down.

After eating jerky and hardtack, Jake and the others stretched out with their heads on the saddles. Their horse blankets covered them. Jessica turned toward Jake. He watched fire shadows bounce off her handsome face. Blackie put an arm on Susan. She grasped his hand and squeezed.

The next morning just before first light, the Apaches stirred, got up, and threw blankets on their ponies. Jake made coffee and passed out jerky. The Apaches ate quickly; Maco signaled everyone to mount up. They rode south at a good clip. The morning was still cool.

The day passed quickly. Maco led the way following tracks of the Mexican's shod horses and his own unshod ponies. That night they camped close to Mexico's border.

"Tomorrow we will be in their country." Maco stood near Jake.

"There may be patrols," Jake cautioned.

"You and one of my warriors will ride first."

"Right—two, three miles ahead should be enough."

Maco narrowed his eyes. "Maybe more."

"If the Mexicans show up, we'll have plenty of time to warn you." Jake started to move away. "Tell your brave—we'll head out at first light."

CHAPTER TWENTY EIGHT

Jake awakened before dawn, grabbed some coffee from a pot left by the fire. A few minutes later, he woke the brave who would go with him. First light was just beginning to spread across the Mexican sky.

As Jake and the brave rode out, Maco woke from a restless sleep. He prodded his warriors and the three White-Eyes awake.

Jake and the brave rode ahead three or four miles following the Mexicans' tracks. The desert, flat and sandy, heated as the sun rose in the cloudless sky. The low, jagged hills on each side of them could conceal the enemy, but the tracks led southwest toward the distant Sierra Madre Mountains.

Maco and the rest of the party were on the trail now.

"What if they're all dead?" Jessica asked.

"They won't be," Susan Blackhawk said. "The Mexicans will keep them for slaves or sell them to the Comancheros or Yaquis."

Blackie rode close. "The Yaquis could attack us."

"Very possible," Susan said.

Jessica adjusted her hat. "Maco must know that."

"He rides ahead like he does," Blackie said. "I've been watching him."

"That's why he sent Jake ahead," Susan said.

Maco, in the lead, searched the hills and desert for traces of the enemy—any enemy. His rifle, out of its sheath, was held ready.

Jake and the brave, a few miles ahead, came to a sudden rise in the trail as it narrowed between tree-laden hills. Jake raised a hand to halt the brave and reached for his field glass. He dismounted, approached the crest, and scanned the area ahead. In a small grove of trees, a dozen or so renegade Mexicans sat around a water hole. Apache women and children were tied to trees. Apache ponies were also tethered to trees. Jake hurried back to the brave, told him, best he could, what he had seen, and motioned him to ride for Maco and the others. Jake would wait there.

Maco saw the brave galloping toward him and stopped. When the warrior arrived, Maco raised a hand. "Where is the white man?"

"He is on the trail waiting. He sent me. Mexicans camped other side of a hill."

Maco signaled and kicked his pinto in the sides. The others followed his fast gait.

When they saw Jake, Maco slowed, reined up by him.

"Your women, children, and ponies are over that rise." Jake pointed.

Maco raised his rifle. "We must take them back—kill all the Mexicans."

"There's about double them than us. Best we wait until dark."

"No." Maco pumped his rifle into the air. "I want to see their faces when I take their scalps."

Jessica put a hand to her mouth. "Oh . . ."

"What's your plan?" Jake asked.

"The women stay here. My warriors will circle behind and to the sides of their camp. You two men and I will attack from the front."

Jake nodded. "Blackie and I will ride ahead of you, to shield you. They will think we're two gringos on the trail."

"That is good. A distraction. Then we attack." Maco motioned to his warriors. "Two of you will ride around the camp and strike from behind when I signal. Two of you will attack from each side of the camp."

After they rode off, Jake and Blackie checked their rifles. Maco waved the women off the trail into the trees.

"We'll give the warriors time to get set," Jake said.

Blackie looked up in the sky. "Still think night would be a better time for this."

"Maco might be right. At night, the Mexicans would post guards. Not in all this afternoon sunshine. It's siesta time."

"Then let's get it over with."

"A few more minutes. Maco will know when."

The Apache sat on his paint with his rifle across his lap. His stare was trained on the horizon. A little while later, he waved Jake and Blackie to move. He followed right behind their horses.

They rode over the hill and down the trail toward the Mexicans' camp. Jake and Blackie, side by side, slowed their stallions to a walk as they neared the encampment. Maco was still hidden behind them.

The Mexican leader, a large, burly man with a big belly and two guns strapped on his waist, watched the strangers approach. He set the bottle he drank from down and wiped his mouth with the back of his right hand. *Gringos—what are they doing this far into Mexico? He better wake his comrades from their siesta.*

Before he had a chance to stir his men, Maco swung his horse around Jake and Blackie. He fired two rapid shots, striking the Mexican in the chest and head. The man fell face-first to the sand and lay still. Jake and Blackie charged, firing at the Mexicans as they rose from their blankets. They scattered for cover and their weapons, but Jake and Blackie's shots hit their targets and some of the Mexicans fell to earth, bleeding and still. Maco's warriors stormed into the camp on war ponies killing anyone in sight. The Apache women and children cringed against the trees until Maco rode to them and cut them free. Then he whirled and assaulted the remaining Mexicans.

In less than a half-hour, the fight was over. The Apaches, Jake, and Blackie surveyed the death scene and gathered the freed prisoners around them.

"You are safe now," Maco said. "Soon we will ride back to our stronghold."

"Better round up the horses." Jake turned Sam.

Maco stopped him. "First we take scalps."

"You sure?"

"The Mexicans must never capture our people again. They need to see what happens if they do." Maco dismounted, signaled his braves.

Blackie nudged Jake. "I think he's right."

"Guess so." Jake nodded. "Their custom."

Later, after picking up weapons and gathering food, the Apache party started back on the trail to New Mexico. Mexican scalps hung from the warriors' horses' manes.

Jake and Blackie turned off the trail and rode to Jessica and Susan Blackhawk's hiding place in the trees on the other side of the rise.

"We heard the gunfire," Jessica said. "I prayed you'd be safe."

"A complete surprise," Jake said. "We hit them hard."

Blackie stopped next to Susan. "That Maco's quite the warrior."

"Yes, he is a strong leader." She looked up to him.

"A real killer," Jake said.

"But a proud man." Blackie swung Ace around. "We better catch up to him."

The others urged their horses behind Blackie and soon caught up with the Apaches.

Maco held up a hand, greeted them. "We are in Yaqui territory. Must be on the alert."

"Maybe I better ride point again." Jake spurred Sam next to Maco.

"Good idea. Do you want a brave with you?"

"I can handle it." Jake took off in a gallop."

A few miles down the trail, Jake slowed. In the hills to the west a column of smoke rose into the sky. *Yaquis!* He turned Sam around, headed back to Maco and the others.

Maco halted everyone when he saw Jake riding hard toward them.

"Smoke! Off to the west in the hills." Jake and Sam slid to a stop.

"Yaquis?" Maco looked up the trail.

"Too far to see from here."

"Yaquis don't send signals. They attack."

Jake pulled on his reins. "I just saw smoke."

Maco pointed to Jake, Blackie, Jessica, and Susan. "You four take the trail north. The rest of us will cut to the east, go around."

"And if the Yaquis attack us?" Jake asked.

"My warriors and I will come."

Jake backed Sam away and turned. "All right. You may be right. Might not be Yaquis."

"If it is, they want women." Maco glanced at Jessica and Susan."

"I'll remember that." Jake kicked Sam in the sides. "Come on, Blackie. Bring the women."

CHAPTER TWENTY NINE

Jake and Blackie rode in front of the two women as they proceeded north toward the border. Jake kept glancing to the hills west of them. Heavier smoke rose from the hills.

Jake took out his field glass. "That's Yaquis all right.'

"Should we make a run for it?" Blackie asked.

"Maco wanted us to flush 'em."

"We're doin' a good job of it. Look!"

A large cloud of dust moved toward them.

Jake looked east. No sign of Maco and his warriors. "Time to hightail it now." He kicked Sam into a gallop. "Come on!"

Susan and Jessica followed him. Blackie brought up the rear.

"There's sand dunes up ahead," Jake said. "Make a stand there."

The dust cloud cleared and rampaging Yaquis rode hard and straight for the four riders.

Jake was the first one behind a sand dune and jumped off Sam with his rifle. He fired at the closest Indian, knocked him off his horse. Blackie and the two women rode in.

"Get down," Jake called. "Take cover."

Blackie grabbed his rifle, pointed to Jessica and Susan. "Get your guns."

They huddled behind Blackie when more Yaquis charged.

Blackie shot one of the Indians who galloped over the sand dune. "Must be twenty of them."

"Maco better get here pretty quick." Jake ripped off another shot at a charging Yaqui.

The Indians circled the sand dune now, firing at the two men, but not at the women.

"They want women all right," Jake said.

Blackie blasted away. "Gonna have to kill me to get 'em."

"Don't waste your bullets."

"Maco ought to be coming."

"Just in case he doesn't." Jake took aim, shot another Yaqui.

Two Indians jumped off their ponies behind another sand dune and crawled toward Susan and Jessica. The women faced the other way and did not see them. Jake and Blackie were busy warding off the front-attacking warriors.

Susan Blackhawk turned just as one of the Yaquis grabbed her around the neck. "Help! Blackie!"

The Indian started pulling her backward. She dropped her gun, tried to tear free of his grip, but he was too strong.

Blackie whirled around. "Susan!" He whipped his rifle up for a shot, but the warrior blocked his aim with Susan.

She kicked at her assailant, but his grip tightened. Blackie moved closer as the warrior backed up with Susan as his shield.

"Susan. Relax. Try to relax—he may loosen his hold." Blackie waved his left hand.

Susan went limp, but the Yaqui kept tugging her backward toward another sand dune.

Jessica, who had crouched in the sand, suddenly jerked up and ran at the warrior. She was intercepted by the other Indian and knocked to the ground. Jake fired at him, but missed. Blackie lunged for the Yaqui who held Susan. Another Indian popped up on top of the back mound and launched a lance at Blackie. It struck him in the chest and dropped him. Jake fired from his hip and killed the Indian. Susan screamed. A mass of Yaquis converged on Jake and he went down under the attack.

As the warriors approached Jake and the women with drawn knives, Maco and his Apaches thundered over the sand dunes firing rifles and throwing lances. The Yaquis on horseback, who were not hit or killed, turned and tried to ride away. Maco's braves chased them down, shot or stabbed them.

Maco leaped off his pinto, ran at the Indian who held Susan Blackhawk. He brandished his knife above his head and thrust it into the warrior's neck.

Jake scrambled to his feet, sprang at the Yaqui holding Jessica. The warrior let go of her and ducked. Jake flew over him, but somersaulted to his feet. The Indian drew his knife, rushed at Jake. He sidestepped, pulled his gun, and shot the attacker.

When Maco dropped Susan's assailant, he turned to help her up. A Yaqui threw a lance at him, pierced his back. Maco fell face down. She bolted to him just as Jake put a bullet in the Indian.

"Jake—Blackie and Maco, they are both dead!" Susan cradled Maco in her arms.

Jessica kneeled over Blackie. "He's pretty bad. Better have a look."

Jake looked down at Blackie's limp body with the lance protruding from his chest. Blood seeped from the wound onto the sand; his eyes had the blank stare of a dead man. "Blackie—she's safe. You saved her."

He never moved, but a slight grin crossed his lips. Then it was gone and so was he.

"Oh, Blackie . . ." Jessica hugged his head.

Jake took off his hat. "He was a good man."

Susan let go of Maco, moved to Blackie. She began wailing in Cheyenne.

Jake bent over Maco, stared at his labored breathing. The Apaches gathered around him, some still on their ponies. They shifted back and forth as Jake cut at the lance in Maco's back with his Bowie knife.

Susan and Jessica came over to help.

"When I pull this out" Jake said, "we'll have to stop the bleeding."

"I've got something." Jessica looked for her horse. "In my saddlebags." She walked over, reached in, and pulled out a blouse.

"This is gonna hurt." Jake pressed on Maco's back.

"I don't think he hears you," Jessica said.

"Good. Susan you help. Hold his head. Jessica—grab his legs."

Susan held him in her arms. "He can't die—like Blackie did."

"Here we go." Jake took hold of the lance and slowly pulled until he saw the blade.

Jessica squeezed Maco's legs. "Won't that blade rip him apart?"

"Not if I'm careful." Jake twisted it until it came free.

Blood flowed out of the wound. Jessica stuffed her blouse into the hole and pressed down.

"Good," Jake said, "that should stop the bleeding, but he needs a doctor."

Jessica looked up. "There's no doctor around here."

"I know. We need the Apaches to gather some desert herbs and pack his wound."

Susan Blackhawk gazed into Maco's blank face. "I will tell them." She laid his head on the sand and motioned the warriors around her.

"What about Blackie?" Jessica asked.

Jake turned. "We'll have to bury him."

"He has no family."

"Then it doesn't matter where he rests."

Jessica's face twisted. "That sounds pretty harsh."

"Look—I liked him. Sorry that he's gone, but I would want him to do the same for me."

"I—I guess you're right."

Susan came back. "The braves will find some herbs."

"After we bury Blackie, we'll make a travois for Maco."

"I grieve for Blackie so his spirits will not wander." Susan's voice wavered.

Jake sought her eyes. "His spirits should be happy. He died fighting for you."

"I will miss him."

"Yeah—so will I." Jake saw the moisture in her eyes. "He would want you to take Ace, his stallion."

Susan smiled. "A grand gift. I shall treasure him."

After the Apaches brought back herbs, Susan crushed and mashed them with water, then packed the mixture into Maco's wound. She wrapped Jessica's blouse around him and turned him face up.

He blinked, opened his eyes just enough to see her smiling at him. He raised his right hand, did not speak. His vision of her was like the first day when he came upon her at the pool— a shining beauty.

"We must take you home," she said. "It will be a long, hard trip. When you need rest, let us know."

He tried to rise up to her, but the pain in his back held him captive. *He had learned pain growing up from an Apache boy to become an Apache warrior. Long days alone in the desert taught him survival and skills. He would not give in to pain. This Cheyenne beauty before him could only inspire him.*

Maco's warriors dug a grave in the soft sand with their hands and knives. They placed Blackie's body into the hole and after Jake said some words over him they filled in his grave. Jessica cried. Susan Blackhawk wailed in her grief.

Jake sent a brave past the sand dunes to fetch two tree branches so he could make a travois for Maco. He threw horse blankets over the poles and tied them down. Then he sent the Apaches for the women, children, and horses. *They must continue the journey home.*

CHAPTER THIRTY

The weary party trudged through the hot desert, crossed the border into New Mexico, and headed north. Susan Blackhawk rode Blackie's stallion, Ace, next to Maco. He tossed in and out of consciousness on the travois pulled by one of the Apache ponies.

Jake rode at the head of the column, always alert for danger.

At night when they camped, Susan attended to Maco, feeding him, giving him water, repacking his wound. He did not speak to her, but when conscious kept watching her movements.

After two more days ride, the party arrived at a point where the trail turned west toward the mountains and east toward Adobe Crossing.

Jessica rode up next to Jake. "Do we turn back to town here?"

He looked at her for a moment. "I'm headin' west. California's still my goal."

"Do you want my company?"

"Sure—if you're prepared for a long, hard ride."

She sighed. "I've been through a lot since we met. How much tougher can it be?"

He smiled. "You never know."

"Then I'm going with you."

"Good. We'll ride with the Apaches til they turn off for their stronghold."

"What about Susan Blackhawk?"

"You ask her. She may want to stay with her people."

"Her people are the Cheyenne."

"I mean Indians."

"I'll ask her." She rode back to Maco's travois.

Susan walked Ace next to Maco.

"How's he doing?" Jessica asked.

Susan looked up. "It will take time."

"He's a strong man."

"Yes—that is what keeps him alive."

Jessica smiled. "And your care."

"Thank you."

"Jake and I talked. We're heading for California. Want to know if you're coming?"

Susan's face turned downward. "I thought I might—until Blackie was killed. Now, Maco needs me. I cannot leave him."

"Don't you want to go back to your people?"

"The Apache are my people now." She peeked at Maco's wound.

"I understand." Jessica turned her horse, rode back to Jake.

Jake turned to her. "Well . . .?"

"She can't leave Maco."

"That settles that. Probably for the best."

"You were right. The Apache are her people now."

"She can't go wrong there. A strong and proud tribe— digging out a life in this sparse land while two countries and renegade Indians try to destroy them."

"I admire them very much."

"Even though they took you captive?"

Yes—even that." She looked away.

Jake slowed Sam, swung him around. "Better tell Maco we're breakin' off west when they turn north for their stronghold."

"Let's hope we don't run into any more Comanches."

Jake trotted toward Maco's travois. "Yeah, let's hope."

Susan Blackhawk glanced up when Jake approached. "He is in and out."

"I wanted to tell him we're headin' west when the Apaches turn toward their camp."

"I will tell him when he wakes."

"You sure you want to stay with him?"

"Yes, I must."

"You're a good women, Susan Blackhawk."

She gazed into his eyes. "Thank you, Jake."

He turned, spurred Sam toward the lead again.

Another two days ride and the column of Apaches turned toward the foothills of their mountains. Jake and Jessica waved as they faded away.

"Well, we're on our own now," she said.

"Should be an interesting trip." Jake pulled the tip of his hat down.

They rode side by side into the afternoon sun. That night they camped near the Gila River, north of Lordsburg.

"So far, so good." Jessica pulled her saddle, set it close to their fire.

Jake picketed the two horses to nearby trees and brought his saddle back to the fire. "Not much for supper tonight—a little jerky. Tomorrow I'll try to kill us some game."

"Jerky's fine with me. With all that's happened, I lost my appetite." Jessica sat against her saddle.

"There's plenty of water and the weather's pretty warm."

"Thank goodness. That thunderstorm we had when we escaped from the Apache stronghold was bad."

"It was, but we survived." He looked at her. "Seems you and I had a kiss that night."

She grinned. "We did, didn't we."

"It was nice."

"Nice? Yeah, nice and short-lived."

Jake fumbled with his saddle blanket. "Did you want it to last longer?"

"Yes."

"Too bad we were busy fighting off the Apaches."

Jessica laughed. "There are priorities, I guess."

"Just life or death."

"We'll just have to try it again sometime."

"Sometime? Look up there." He pointed to the sky. "A million stars—and a sliver of a moon."

"She gazed upward. "It is pretty."

"And so are you."

"Why thank you, Jake."

He moved toward her. "What if sometime is now?"

"I think I'd like that."

He threw his hat back at his saddle and slid down next to her. Jessica lifted her face to him and he cupped it in his hands. Holding her close for a few moments, Jake slowly sought her lips with his and pressed tenderly.

They held their kiss until she broke away for a breath.

"That was a good sometime." She wheezed.

He smiled. "Sure was."

"What now?"

"That's up to you."

"Why me?"

"I think the lady should say what's next."

"Really—well, I liked that kiss. Maybe we should try it again."

"I'm for that." He took her in his arms and this time his kiss was more passionate.

She responded, drew closer to him, and cupped his hands to her breasts. Their fervor intensified to the point where they started to claw at each other's clothes. Jake was just about to rip off his gunbelt when he heard a growl. He turned from Jessica and stared into the glaring eyes of a large wolf, a few feet away.

CHAPTER THIRTY ONE

"Jessica, don't move." He held her down with his left hand and dropped his right hand to his gun.

More growls broke the night air as three other wolves circled the camp. Jake gripped his gun's butt and slid his fingers to the trigger. The wolf closest to them let out a loud snarl and charged. Jake pulled the gun out of his holster and fired point blank at the wolf. The animal's head exploded as the bullet penetrated it. Jake swung around, shot another wolf running at them. The two remaining wolves retreated to the nearby trees, but did not leave the area.

Jessica wiggled free from Jake's hold and inched up on one elbow. "Are they gone?" She squinted into the darkness.

"Not all of them. Better stay down." He watched the two pairs of eyes poking out from the trees.

Jessica heard the low growling and hugged the ground. "How many did you kill?"

"Two—there's two left."

"Maybe I can reach our rifles." She started to crawl toward the tree stump where they had placed them.

"Easy now. Real slow."

The howling grew louder from the wolves. They paced back and forth in the trees. Jake kept his pistol trained on them. Susan almost reached the rifles when one of the wolves charged. She dashed the last few feet, grabbed a rifle, and threw it to Jake. He whirled, fired at the attacking animal. The shot dropped the wolf a few feet from them. Jessica picked up the other rifle and plopped next to Jake, ready to shoot.

"One to go." He kept his eyes on the woods.

Jessica looked at the dwindling fire. "Flames going out."

"You watch where I'm pointing. I'll put more branches on it." He moved away.

She rose up, leaned against a saddle, and aimed her rifle toward the woods.

After throwing more wood on the fire, Jake stalked the last wolf. He circled around the right side of the clearing and slipped into the trees. Jessica watched him, cocked her rifle. She jerked when two shots barked, but relaxed as Jake walked back to the fire.

"We're all right now," he said.

"Until the next time." She grinned.

He sat next to her. "Now, where were we?"

"I think I've had all the excitement I can stand for tonight."

He smiled at her. "Then I suggest we get some sleep."

The next morning, Jake woke before Jessica and made some coffee. The sky was clear with a slight breeze. The coffee's aroma drifted toward Jessica.

She stirred, opened her eyes. "That smells very inviting."

"About the best I can do."

"I could cook bacon and eggs—if we had any."

"Sorry. This'll have to do this morning."

"Maybe today we'll find a town."

"Maybe. We better get a pack horse, too." He poured her a cup of coffee.

She took a swallow. "Ummm—that's good."

After they each had another cup of coffee, they saddled up and headed west again.

* * * *

The Apache warriors herded the horses into the canyon below their stronghold. Maco, on a travois, and the women and children followed close behind. Susan Blackhawk rode Ace beside him, all the time keeping watch over him.

When they arrived at the camp, Susan dismounted and helped carry Maco into his wickiup. They laid him on a buffalo robe close to the fire pit. She summoned the Medicine Man after hearing Maco's labored breathing.

164

The shaman arrived in his traditional attire and began his chanting, spreading hands over Maco's body, and dancing. Susan stood to the side and watched. Maco did not move during the ceremony.

An hour later, the Medicine Man said his last chant and walked out of the wickiup. Maco opened his eyes slightly; Susan kneeled beside him and held his head in her hands. He opened his mouth, but did not speak. She gave him a few sips of water from a gourd. He blinked his eyes and she dabbed cool water on his forehead.

"You will get well, Maco. I will care for you." She drew him close to her bosom.

He moved his lips, but nothing came out and he gazed at her.

"I must turn you now. The shaman left new herbs to heal your wound." She rolled him on his side and applied the new medicine to his back.

Maco grunted when she touched his wound and stiffened. His face twisted with the pain.

"I know your pain is great, but I will stay with you until you are healed." She turned him gently on his back.

His large black eyes did not leave her. She daubed more water on his forehead with one hand and stroked his thick hair with the other. He relaxed, closed his eyes, and fell into a tranquil sleep.

"There now, you rest—get well and strong again." She bent her cheek to his.

When Susan awakened the next morning, her head was on Maco's chest, her face upturned to his. He stirred slightly, but did not waken. His right arm lay across her shoulder. She inched up, shook the stiffness from her body. His breathing was smooth and the pain seemed gone from his face. Her stare lingered on his rugged features, the high cheekbones, well formed nose, strong jaws, and firm-closed lips.

How would those lips feel on hers like Blackie had taught her? She wondered. *Surely he would want her. Their passion was felt since the first meeting at the pool, but they traveled other paths with all the attacks upon them. He was strong and brave. She felt his aura even as he lay near death. Was this the start of the white man's love?* She backed away, but continued to gaze at the great warrior.

Maco's eyes opened as Susan slipped out of the wickiup. He stared at the entrance flap. *Had Usen, the Giver of Life, taken him and returned him to the tribe? Was the beautiful Cheyenne maiden a spirit of his? He knew not what to think. He had been in raids, in fights—the Comanches, Mexicans, Yaquis—brother with the White-Eyes, yet*

now all he saw was the woman who tended him. How many horses would it take to make her his wife? But who would he offer them to? She had no family. Maco closed his eyes, drifted back to sleep.

* * * *

Jake and Jessica followed the Gila River southwest between mountain ranges until it turned northwest. It was past mid-day and hot.

"We should rest here," Jake said. "Water the horses."

Jessica took off her hat, wiped her forehead. "Are we going to follow the river?"

"According to the old timers in town, the Gila goes north here, but swings back south and west on the other side of the desert."

"How far is it?"

"Don't know exactly." He gazed straight westward. "It's a ways."

"Looks pretty hot and desolate to me." She put her hat back on.

"You're right, but we can load up on water here, rest, and go on after sundown."

"What about food? We haven't seen a town yet today."

"Closest town is San Carlos—at least two days ride from here."

"Are there more Apaches that way?"

Jake turned to her. "This is all Apache territory."

"So, what will we eat?" Her voice had a slight tremble.

"I'll find some small game."

"You mean snakes—lizards?"

"Maybe, but there should be rabbits, quail along the way."

"A roasted quail sounds good."

"Right now we get jerky." He dug into his saddlebags and gave her two strips.

"Thank you." She saluted him with her hat.

Jake smiled. "You're welcome—for now."

After the sun started down behind the far mountains, Jake and Jessica saddled up and headed west across the Gila River.

"It'll be a bit cooler tonight," Jake said.

"Isn't that when the critters come out?"

He grinned. "Yeah, stay on your pinto."

She did not return a smile. "I will, thank you."

They rode into the sunset without many words exchanged until night's blanket covered the land. The moon rounded from the sliver of a few nights before and provided enough light for Jake to lead the way.

Sometime after midnight, Jake noticed Jessica's head bobbing up and down. "We better stop the rest of the night."

"What? Oh . . ." She jerked up, sat straight in her saddle.

"You're falling asleep."

"Just resting my eyes."

"Pull up now." He reined Sam.

She stopped next to him, closed her eyes again.

Jake dismounted, reached her just as she slipped off her horse into his arms.

Jessica opened her eyes. "Jake—where are we?"

"Middle of the desert."

"I'm tired."

"I know." He carried her to a small mound of sand.

She shook her head. "But the critters."

"I'll build a fire." He tied the horses to a manzanita bush, then gathered some brush.

The flames lit up the area and Jake pulled their saddles, set them around the fire.

He placed their blankets on the sand near Jessica. She stretched out on one with her head on her saddle. Jake lay next to her.

"Good night," he said.

Sleepily, she turned toward him. "Good night." Her eyes closed in a few moments, then she heard the rattle.

CHAPTER THIRTY TWO

Jake whipped out his gun, shot the snake's head off as it sprang at Jessica.

She stared at the rattler as it quivered in the sand next to her blanket. "You seem to always be rescuing me."

"Glad to do it, Miss." He grinned.

"Oh, you . . ." *He might be funnin' with her, but she was glad he was around.*

Jake holstered his gun. "Better get some sleep." He threw the snake's head and body away from their camp. "Now the coyotes won't bother us."

"I've had enough critters for one night." She turned toward him.

He piled more brush on the fire and returned next to Jessica. "You'll feel better in the morning."

"Sure."

* * * *

Later the same day after they arrived at the Apache stronghold, Maco woke up again. His eyes focused much better. Susan Blackhawk sat next to him with a wet cloth in her hands.

"You look stronger," she said.

He blinked, reached for her hand. "Usen is not ready for me yet."

"Let us pray it will be a long, long time." She took his hand.

"Because you care for me, it will be."

"Yes, I care for you." She blushed.

He squeezed her hand. "When I am well we will walk and ride like we were spoken for."

"I would like that."

"Now I will sit up."

"Let me help you." She pulled his hand forward. "I will pack new herbs into your wound."

Maco adjusted to a sitting position and bent forward. Susan changed the dressing.

"After food," he said, "I will summon my warriors."

"Yes, I will get you food." She left the wickiup.

When she came back, Maco ate more than he had since he was wounded. "I can feel the strength returning."

"Good. Should I call the warriors now?"

"Yes. We need to talk."

She started to leave, but he stopped her by raising a hand. "Why is it no Cheyenne warrior ever came for you?"

Susan turned. "I had no young brave. Most of our camp was killed when the Comanches took me."

"But they tried to get you back from me."

"The Comanches want captives for slaves or trade. No warrior wanted me for himself."

"They did not know a treasure right before their eyes."

Susan looked at him for a few minutes. "I am glad you think me that." Then she walked out of the wickiup.

After meeting with his warriors, Maco was helped outside and sought Susan Blackhawk. She finished washing clothes and walked back to camp.

"It is good to see the sky again," he said.

Surprised that he stood outside his wickiup, she set the basket of clothes down. "I am glad you are up, but you should not overdo it."

"Each day I feel my strength returning. Soon we can ride."

"That will be nice, but now I think you should go back inside and rest."

"Is this a wife speaking?" He let a slight grin cross his lips.

"I should like to be a wife someday. Now go into the wickiup."

"Yes, a wife."

A few days later, Maco woke early and threw blankets on his black and white pinto and Susan's Ace. He led them to the wickiup and woke Susan. "Today is a good day for riding."

She stretched, rubbed her eyes. "Are you sure you are strong enough?"

"Yes. You have given me strength with your care."

"Then, I will ride with you."

"We can go to the desert below."

"The desert is beautiful in the early morning."

He looked longingly at her. "As you are."

Susan felt his stare; a flushing spread over her cheeks. She turned Ace, headed out of the camp at a walk. Maco followed on his big paint.

In the foothills above the desert, Maco stopped, gazed at the beauty. "Before the white man there was plenty of game for our wickiups."

"It was the same on the plains. My father was a trapper. My Cheyenne mother told me of the buffalo, deer, and elk."

"I am afraid more and more white men will come."

"Yes. Our way of life will never be the same." Her voice trembled.

"I will not give in as long as I can fight." He raised his rifle to the sky.

"It is good you are like you are."

"I can only be what is inside me." He urged his pinto downward.

Susan followed, but stopped a few minutes later when she saw a dust cloud below and east in the desert. "Look."

Maco squinted, put a hand over his eyes to shield the sun, and looked hard and long. "We must wait until it gets closer."

They kicked their horses in the sides and rode toward a group of trees.

Below, in the desert, a shave-tail lieutenant led a troop of cavalry toward Maco and Susan Blackhawk. "Sergeant, our scouts say the Apaches are holed up in those mountains northwest of here."

"Yes sir, that's what they say."

"We will forge ahead right up that canyon and attack their camp."

"Yes sir."

"The reports say it's not a big camp."

"Yes sir." The sergeant dropped back into line.

Maco watched the cavalry turn and head for the canyon leading to his stronghold. "I will warn the camp. You stay here where you will be safe." He spurred his stallion and galloped up the hill.

"Be careful," Susan whispered after him.

Maco thundered into the stronghold, called everyone together. "The soldiers are coming. They will kill us if we do not kill first. The warriors and I will hide in the rocks. Some of you women and older children will dress as warriors to fool them. The elders must stay in their wickiups. When the soldiers attack, scatter and we warriors will strike from the rocks."

The cavalry troop rode up the canyon in single file. The Apache lookouts watched them until they got close to the stronghold. Then the scouts ran to Maco, told him how near the soldiers were.

The lieutenant smelled the campfires, halted, and lined up his men for the attack. The bugler sounded the charge and the troops kicked their horses. They rode into the camp with rifles blazing in all directions. The women and children scattered like Maco had told them, some to the rocks, some to the wickiups. Maco and his warriors discharged a volley of bullets from their rifles dropping the soldiers as they rode by.

The lieutenant realized the ambush and recalled his troops. They raced back to the stronghold's entrance to regroup.

"We can't see 'em," the sergeant said.

"There's more than we were told." The lieutenant held his horse.

"We need another troop."

"You're right, Sergeant, but right now I'm sending a dispatch back to the fort."

"I'll go."

The lieutenant paused a moment. "All right—take two troopers with you. Tell the colonel what we ran into."

"Yes sir." The sergeant picked two men and rode off.

A short time later, the sergeant came back leading a black stallion with a woman on its back. "Lieutenant—lookee what I found—a Cheyenne squaw."

CHAPTER THIRTY THREE

"What's a Cheyenne doin' in Apache Country?"

"Don't know. She was hiding in some trees."

"Do you speak her language?"

"Tried—she won't say anything."

"Where are the troopers?"

"Sent 'em on to the fort."

The lieutenant surveyed the woman closely. "What are we gonna do with her?"

"She may belong to one of those Apache bucks." The sergeant pulled on Ace's reins.

"Might be good for a powwow with them."

"Yes sir."

Susan Blackhawk sat on Ace, listened to the two men, but watched the canyon for signs of Maco.

The Apache scouts watched the soldiers from their lookout spots. They saw Susan Blackhawk brought up the hill on her horse. They raced back to camp and told Maco.

"The blue coats have captured your Cheyenne woman."

Maco's face dropped. "How could this happen? I left her in a hiding place."

"She is on her horse with her hands tied."

Maco reached for his rifle. "We ride—kill the soldiers—get her back."

The other warriors gathered around him with lances and rifles.

"We will attack from three sides. Some of you will stay in the rocks. I will strike from the west and the rest from the east." Maco led them out of the camp.

The lieutenant and his men sat on their horses, waited for reinforcements. The sergeant held Ace's reins and watched Susan Blackhawk. She gazed up the canyon at the rocks.

Maco motioned his warriors to the east and to the center of the canyon. He and a few braves rode west.

Some of the troopers dismounted and stood in groups. The lieutenant straddled his horse and the sergeant shifted from side to side in his saddle. One of the troopers walked up the hill a ways and stood beside his horse.

No one heard the thud until the trooper hit the ground with an arrow in his back. Then came the yelps and war cries of the attacking Apaches. Several troopers fell from rifle wounds as Maco and the other warriors struck death. The sergeant turned just as Susan dug her knees into Ace and he bounded away from the cavalry. She grabbed Ace's mane with her tied hands and raced up the canyon. The sergeant looked on with his mouth wide open until a bullet sent him to the dirt. The lieutenant fought valiantly, but was overwhelmed by Maco, who held a rifle to his throat.

"Tell your men to stop fighting." Maco pushed the barrel tighter against the soldier's skin.

The lieutenant, wide-eyed, tensed with the warning. "Then you will kill us."

"I could kill you now." Maco jabbed him again.

"All right." He eased the rifle away from his throat. "Cease fire!"

Not all the remaining troopers heard him. "Cease fire!"

This time he was heard and the battle stopped.

"This is our land." Maco faced the lieutenant. "You must not try to take us anymore."

"This land belongs to the United States. I only follow orders." His voice was defiant.

Maco eyed him closely. "You are brave for one so young. Maybe I should test your strength."

The lieutenant stood his ground. "That's up to you."

"No!" Susan Blackhawk rode back. "Maco, you are not strong enough to fight."

He turned. "When does a woman tell Maco he is not strong enough?"

"When she knows."

Maco paused, studied her with penetrating eyes. "You may be right." He felt a twinge of pain in his back.

"It has been not so long since you were badly wounded," Susan said.

"We shall see." He turned to the lieutenant. "You go now. If we meet again, your fate will not be so tame."

"We'll go." He signaled his troops, then saluted Maco. *He had not known an Apache who let his quarry live. He would remember this man.*

Maco did not acknowledge the lieutenant's salute. He pointed his rifle to the east.

As the soldiers trotted off, Susan drew near to Maco. "It was a wise decision."

"If it was not, I will kill them all."

"I hope you will not have to."

Maco reached for her hand. "You are safe now."

"Thanks to you." She took his hand.

* * * *

Jake and Jessica rode west a ways north of Tucson. The heat radiated from the desert's parched floor scorched the riders as the sun beat down.

"We need a water hole," Jake said.

Jessica shook her canteen. "Mine's almost empty."

"Listen!" Jake reined up Sam. "Gunfire."

"I hear it." She stopped. "Where?"

"Over that rise up ahead. Come on." He kicked Sam in the sides.

Jessica followed.

As they rode over the mound, Indians raided a herd of cattle. Two wagons stood parked in the sand with cowboys shooting from behind them.

Jake handed Jessica his rifle. "Ride to the wagons." He pulled his pistol, started firing as he rode in.

They found an opening through the scattered cattle and Indians and halted behind the wagons.

The trail boss stopped shooting, turned to Jake. "They jumped us—didn't see them coming."

"They're Chiricahua Apaches." Jake leaped off Sam. "Give them some of the herd, they'll go away." An arrow flew past him and he shot the warrior.

The Apaches attacked until the cowboys cut out part of the herd and sent them toward the warriors. The raiders hustled the cattle away without further bloodshed.

"That's all they wanted," Jake holstered his gun.

The trail boss cradled his rifle. "Thanks. We're driving from Fort Smith—all the way to California. Thought this old Butterfield Stage trail was safe."

"You're deep in Apache Territory. We had a few run-ins ourselves."

Jessica, who had hugged one of the wagons, dismounted and walked toward the two men. The tall, rangy trail boss, in his thirties, studied her until she caught his eye, then he turned away.

She walked past him to Jake. "Could they have been part of Maco's band?"

"I don't think so, but they're Chiricahuas."

The trail boss moved closer. "And who might this young lady be?"

"I'm Jessica." She gave him an annoyed look.

He held out a hand. "Tom Hardy."

She did not take it, but Jake did. "Jake Harwood."

"Thanks for helping us," Tom said.

"Didn't do much," Jake said, "but you saved us. We're near out of water."

"Better fill your canteens from that barrel over there." Tom pointed.

Jessica walked back to her horse, grabbed her canteen, and filled it. She took several swallows of water. Jake followed her and had his fill.

"You're welcome to ride along with us," Tom said. "We could use the extra guns."

Jessica turned. "What do you think, Jake? Sounds like a good idea."

"I suppose we could—for a few miles at least."

"This desert is pretty hot and dry."

"There'd be water and plenty beef."

Jessica grinned. "And maybe rest without wolves and snakes."

"Or interruptions." Now Jake smiled.

"We'll have to see about that."

Tom, the trail boss, stood silent not catching all of their banter.

"We'll take you up on the offer," Jake said.

"Good. Now there's miles to cover before nightfall." Tom mounted his horse, rode to the head of the herd.

That evening, the drive stopped near the San Pedro River. The cattle watered in the river, as the cowboys kept alert. Jake and Jessica settled in by one of the wagons. The trail boss and three men took the first watch.

After a good meal of fresh beef, Jake pulled their saddles and set them side by side. "It's cooling down a bit."

"Thank goodness," Jessica said, "I won't mind a blanket tonight."

"Better turn in then." He spread their blankets on the sand.

"Good night." She lay down.

"Yeah, good night." He turned toward her.

Jessica did not go right to sleep. She stared at the starry sky.

"What are you thinking?" Jake asked.

"I was just wondering where all this will lead?"

"To the California Gold Country, I hope."

Jessica turned toward him. "I didn't mean that."

Puzzlement crossed Jake's face, "What did you mean?"

"I meant us."

"Oh."

"Was it such a surprise?"

"I guess not. Only that we . . ."

"What? That we've been through so much, there's no time to think about us?"

"Well, things have moved pretty fast since we met."

"I know, but I thought there was something between us."

"I guess there is—it's just—I was married—she ran out—didn't want that to happen again."

Jessica raised up on one elbow. "I know. You told me. But you're not a lawman anymore."

"True, but we keep running into trouble."

"Today's trouble is over now." She inched toward him.

He grinned. "You're right."

"Well?"

He drew her close and gently kissed her mouth.

CHAPTER THIRTY FOUR

They lay in each other's arms for several minutes behind a wagon away from the rest of the camp.

Jessica laughed, softly. "Let's hope no wolves or snakes break this up."

"Don't think they will here, but there are cowboys over there." He pointed to the other side of the camp.

"I don't care about them."

"Good." He kissed her again, caressed her body all over until they broke for air.

"Jake, it's been so long."

"For me too."

They kissed until passion overwhelmed them and fumbled with each other's clothes, then he drew her close, kissed her neck and down to her breasts.

"Jake, I need you so much."

He blended with her until she cried out, flung her arms around his neck, met his lips with hers, and let the heated smoothness of his flesh take her.

* * * *

Maco, Susan Blackhawk, and the other warriors returned to their stronghold. The late afternoon sun started its descent to the horizon.

"I will fix you a fine meal," Susan said.

"That would be good." Maco entered his wickiup.

Susan went to the cooking fire and prepared part of a mule for them. Then she took their meal back to the wickiup.

"This is your favorite food." She handed it to Maco.

"Mule, yes, I forgot we took one from the soldiers." He sat and ate with her.

After their meal, they went for a walk.

"You are a good cook," Maco said. "A fine trait for a wife."

Susan looked up. "A wife?"

"Yes. Did your Cheyenne mother teach you?"

"Some, but I was young when she was killed."

"And the Comanche mother?"

"I watched the Comanche, but they did not teach me."

"And the braves?"

She saw the question on his face. "They stayed away. The chief wanted me pure, to sell to the Mexicans."

"And are you pure?"

Susan looked away. ". . . Yes." *She could not tell him about Blackie.*

"So—who should I see about marriage?"

She turned back to him. "Me."

"How many horses will it cost?"

"I have a horse."

"A very fine black stallion indeed."

"Why do I need more?"

His voice was stern. "It is custom."

"You are all I need."

"Then it is settled."

"Yes."

"I will tell the shaman." He pulled her to him and wrapped his arms around her.

Maco explained to the Medicine Man that he wanted to marry Susan Blackhawk, but she had no living family. They sat in his wickiup.

"You must still offer wealth to her," the shaman said.

Maco rose to his feet. "I will give ten horses."

"Tie them near her wickiup. She will have four days to feed and water them or reject them and you."

"It is understood."

"Good." The Medicine Man left the wickiup.

Susan saw the horses outside her wickiup the next morning. *She knew the custom, but was surprised Maco gave her his best horses. She already had told him he was all she needed.*

Because it was bad form, she would not care for the horses the first day. But on the second day, she would water and feed them and accept Maco as her husband.

The shaman saw she had accepted Maco and called the band together for the three days of the wedding feast.

During the time when Susan cared for the horses, Maco built another wickiup hidden in the trees. On the third night of the feast he and Susan disappeared to their temporary wickiup, eluding the elders.

Maco had made a fire pit in the wickiup and placed buffalo robes around it. When they entered, he started a fire and pointed to the soft robes.

Susan sat down. "This is a fine, soft bed."

"I hope you will like it here with me."

"I will. You are a good, strong man and you are in my heart."

"And you are in mine—since the first time I saw you in the water." He sat next to her.

She put a hand on his shoulder. "No one will bother us here."

"I have hidden our place well."

"What will we do?"

"We will become one—a man and woman joined forever."

Susan nestled close to him. "I will like that."

Maco put an arm around her, squeezed her shoulder. She looked into his dark eyes and saw the fire within. He slid the deerskin dress off her shoulders until it hung from her breasts. Then she slipped off her moccasins and stretched out before him. His chest was already bare and he pulled off his leggings and moccasins. She wiggled out of her dress and lay naked next to him.

"Your body is smooth as a polished stone, but much softer," he said.

She surveyed him. "And yours is hard and muscular as granite."

They turned toward each other and grasped hands. His were callused, hers softer. Their eyes searched each other's body for a long time, marveling in their wonderment.

"You have much beauty," he said, "more than the greatest eagle in flight."

"It is a great honor you think so." She snuggled closer to him.

Maco touched her hip and thigh. She quivered, put her arms around his neck, and pressed her firm breasts to his chest. Now he felt her warmth and pulled her up on his aroused member. She straddled him and pulsated when he entered her moist haven. They lay together a few moments until he could wait no longer and impaled her to exhaustion.

She rolled off him onto her back and lay catching her breath. They lay next to each other for a long time. *Contented, Susan felt his strength. She missed the mouth kisses Blackie had shown her, but knew Maco's heart was full of her. It would be good to have a man all the time—to love—to take care of. She must show him her heart is full of him also.*

CHAPTER THIRTY FIVE

After a short respite, Jake and Jessica joined together again. The first time had been fast, but now they took time exploring each other. When they were finished, they lay close gazing at the stars.

"It finally happened," she said. "I didn't think you'd ever get around to it."

Jake turned to her. "There have been a few obstacles along the way."

"I must say it's been worth the wait." She grinned.

"Glad you think that. Haven't had much practice lately."

She laughed now. "I understand."

"Time should improve our little venture."

"Yes, I'm sure."

They both laughed now.

In the morning, before daybreak, the wranglers woke the camp and started the cattle on the trail. Jake and Jessica rode in front of the wagons. It was a slow and dusty journey until they halted that evening.

After a hearty meal, Jake sat beside Jessica close to their picketed horses.

"Don't know if I want to stay with this drive," he said.

"It is slow."

"I think we should strike out on our own. What do you think?"

She looked at him. "If that's what you want, it's all right with me."

"Still a long way to California."

"But we're still in Apache Country."

"I haven't forgotten that." Jake rose. "I'll tell the trail boss."

Early the next morning, Jake and Jessica struck out alone in front of the cattle drive. They rode at a good pace until noon when the sun scorched the desert trail.

"We'd better find some shade and rest a spell." Jake wiped the sweat from his forehead.

Jessica reined up beside him. "That sun is blazing."

They found a water hole surrounded by trees and unsaddled their horses.

"Stay in the shade," Jake said.

"You don't have to tell me that." She removed her hat.

"I know." He grinned.

"Funny man."

Two hours later, they started out again. Refreshed, their horses responded to the heat and picked up the pace.

That evening it cooled down a bit and they camped by a river. After picketing their horses, they ate and sat by the fire.

"I wonder if Maco has recovered?" Jessica asked.

"I'd say so, by now," Jake said. "He's a strong man."

"That he is. Do you think they got married?"

"You mean Maco and Susan Blackhawk?"

"Yes."

Jake showed surprise. "Didn't know they were that way. Thought she was close to Blackie."

"But he's dead." Her face twisted.

"She'll need a brave."

"No better warrior than Maco."

Jake looked off in the distance. "Too bad we're enemies."

"I didn't think you left if that way."

"Guess we didn't, but we're both cautious around the other."

"Then we're not out of danger yet?"

"This is still Chiricahua Territory."

"When will we be safe?"

"Don't know. California's on the other side of the Colorado River, but there's bandits, cutthroats in the gold country, crooked gamblers—you name it."

Jessica's eyes lowered. "We'd better be smarter."

They pressed on another two weeks without any incidents. As they neared the Colorado River, a violent thunderstorm hit them and swelled the rampaging river. Jake found shelter under a rocky ledge for them. After two days of the storm, the rain stopped, but the river ran fast and high.

"It's still too rough to cross," Jake said.

"Maybe tomorrow." Jessica gazed at the fast-flowing water.

"We'll have to wait it out."

Two days later, Jake decided they could cross the river. Jessica started into the water. Jake followed a short distance behind her. About a fourth of the way across the river, her horse stepped into a hole and threw Jessica into the raging current. She went under, but popped back up and was swept downstream. Jake spurred Sam after her, but she was too far ahead of them. He swung Sam to shore, whipped out his lariat, and galloped downstream. Jessica bobbed up and down, flailed her arms in the air. The current dragged her under; Jake could not see her. He scanned the river until she surfaced again. He tried to rope her, but missed. Her horse swam toward her after he recovered from the fall. Jake tried to rope her again, but missed. As the horse approached her, Jessica grabbed for the saddle. She missed it and the horse swept past her. She lashed out, caught his tail, and hung on.

Jake watched as she pulled herself onto the saddle. He threw the rope again and snared the pinto's neck. The stallion turned toward shore as Jake backed Sam away from the river's edge.

Safe on the eastern bank, Jessica sat on the ground, exhausted. "Thank heaven. Thought I was a goner."

"So did I." Jake patted the big horse on the neck.

"We'll still have to get across."

"The river should slow in a couple of days." Jake scanned the water again.

"Then California?"

"Yeah, California."

Three days later, they crossed the Colorado into California.

Jessica pointed west. "We made it."

Jake turned to her. "The gold fields are north."

"How long will it take us?"
"Couple of weeks."
"Then what?"
Jake smiled. "How 'bout we get married?"
Stunned, Jessica stared at him with her mouth open. "Why not."

About the Author

A pharmacist licensed in three states, Harvey Mendez lives in Southern California with his wife, Ann. He has co-authored a screenplay and has six short stories, two essays, one poem, and seven novels published.

His novel, AMELIA, is a best seller and placed fourth in a national contest and was a finalist in the EPPIE 2003 contest. THE BEAR AND THE BULL won first place in a national contest as a short story in 1986.

He belongs to the Lagunita Writers Group in Laguna Beach, California, the Cherokee Village Writers Guild in Arkansas, and the Claremont Writers' Workshop.